I0628393

OMNITRONW

THE CYBORG CHRONICLES
BOOK 7

PAULINE BAIRD JONES

ISBN: 978-1-962125-20-8

INTRODUCTION

She trusted the cyborg. Can she trust the man?

Tim was once an unstoppable cyborg. Now he's human again—too human, with a body that feels clumsy, emotions he doesn't know how to control, and one scientist he can't get out of his system.

Riina Katala never expected her friendship with Tim to turn into something that keeps her awake at night. But seeing him in his new, flesh-and-blood form stirs feelings she's not ready to face—especially when duty demands she lead a dangerous mission with him at her side.

Their task? Rescue a stranded geologist before his accidental first contact ignites a planetary disaster.

Their risk? Facing the truth about each other while an ominous alien presence darkens the skies above Arroxan Prime.

Caught between duty and desire, Tim and Riina must decide if they can be more than partners—or if the universe has other plans.

From award-winning author Pauline Baird Jones comes a perilously fun, heart-pounding space adventure of love, loyalty, and second chances.

PROLOGUE

Dr. Miles Walker still wasn't sure how his mission to Arroxan Prime had ended up going sideways. He probably should have realized that an Earth geology degree wasn't that much help on another planet, in a whole other galaxy.

But he had tried to follow his orders, but he was a geologist, not a diplomat. It wasn't his fault that *don't make contact* had become *how do I handle contact until someone who knows how to do this first contact thing gets here?*

It had all seemed to simple before he got here. Discover why a millenniums old sensor had turned on, and if possible, turn it off. The only reason he'd been chosen for the mission was because the sensor registered seismic disruptions. The connection between a sensor malfunction and earthquakes was a little thin, but he'd figured they hadn't had anyone else to send.

He'd done what he could to solve the problem but under the heading of "expect the unexpected," his solution might have triggered more problems. Oops. So here he was, stuck on a distant planet, trying to diplomat without starting a war.

Luckily there was an upside.

Miles looked at the upside—Lira Taan—with what he

hoped was a serious and thoughtful expression, one minus the utter terror he felt about possibly screwing things up even more. Or getting dissected as an alien.

"How are your people likely to deal with the knowledge they aren't alone in the universe?" Miles asked.

"It will be fine," Lira's father said, neither looking or sounding convinced that fine would happen.

"How did your world take it?" Lira asked.

Her level of confidence in him was as unsettling as her eyes, her lips, her—he gave himself a shake. So far neither Lira or her father had stated that dissection was off the table. He needed to focus.

Miles noticed Harold shift its feet. It was such a human movement for a robot. Miles resisted the urge to follow its example. He probably shouldn't mention the war that broke out almost immediately upon their Expedition's arrival in the Garradian Galaxy. Or their mostly paranoid movies and television shows.

"It was great," he said. "A real party."

———

Pollin Sollin almost missed it. He was just pushing back his chair when his equipment registered…something.

He stared at the signal. He'd seen the same thing a few days ago. Was it, could it be, a communication signal?

It matched nothing in his database that was associated with Arroxan Prime's standard communications. Could it be…an off-world communication?

He tried to tamp down the surge of hope. He'd been here before. He'd seen what could be communication signals broadcasting at a range not used even by their military. And he had been disappointed time and again.

But….even the signals he broadcast in hopes of reaching

something, or someone, weren't at the range this one registered on his equipment.

He hesitated, then settled back down in front of his broad-casting equipment and dialed his signal up. His finger hovered over the command to send it out into the cosmos. He wasn't supposed to use it. It was dangerous. It was reckless. It was— he pressed it.

1
―――――

Riina Katala stood in the shadows watching Tim—formerly an OmnitronW robot—talking to his physical therapist.

She didn't remember what she'd thought he'd look like. The reality had wiped away all expectations and left her…winded… every time she saw him.

It was disconcerting.

From imposing and towering lethal metal to *this*.

Oh, he had retained his lethal aura, and he still exuded extreme competence. But now it was all packaged into tall, broad, muscled, and *human*. So potently human.

Had she known he had been this good-looking would she have encouraged him to return to his cloned human body? And how had he left this behind? Hadn't he realized…but of course, it hadn't mattered. He'd been a slave of the *Q'uy*.

It wasn't as if he'd had a choice. But, as she often heard the Earth humans say, "Dang, he was pretty."

They'd been friends almost from their first meeting. They had done multiple diplomatic missions together, including the very dangerous one with General Halliwell.

Despite his lethal appearance, she'd felt completely safe with him.

What did she feel now?

Not something that felt safe, that was for sure.

Why did her heart hammer in her chest when she saw him? Why did her face feel hot, and her hands feel cold?

She needed to figure this out before they came face-to-face again. Before they had to leave for their next mission.

She'd dreamt about him last night. She'd been in the hangar bay waiting for him, just like so many times before. The door had slid back and he'd stepped through it. Not the robot. The man.

Their eyes—his human eye—had found her and she'd rocked back on her heels. There'd been a question in there, and he'd held out his hand to her. She'd walked to him, surprised to find she could move. Surprised at how eager she'd been to take his outstretched hand.

His so very human hand had closed around hers and she'd been flooded with a feeling that felt so right that tears had pricked her dream eyes.

She'd woken up shaken and disoriented to find herself alone. She'd flexed the hand he'd held, still feeling the tingle in her skin from the dream contact.

She had thrown back her coverings and gone to get water to drink. It had helped. A little. She'd leaned her head against the cold wall, trying to regain her composure.

Riina was a scientist and she'd always prided herself on her command of her emotions—both before their long sleep and now in this unsettling future she'd landed in.

She liked Tim, the cyborg. Her mind and his had…meshed. They'd made a good team. He could both think logically and break things when things needed to be broken. A smile had flickered on her lips at this thought. She had been mildly infected with the way the people of the Earth Expedition talked.

She should have realized she might have caught other things from them. They were a people who were unabashed about who they were and what they felt a situation required. Their belief in themselves extended from breaking things to, well, romance.

She was sincerely happy for those of her kind who had found happiness with those from the Earth Expedition and others of the former cyborgs. She just didn't know how to reconcile who she'd believed she was and this...surge of emotion that had been infiltrating her mind even before Tim made the decision to migrate from mostly robotic cyborg to mostly human cyborg.

And then there was the other factor.

Tim.

What did he think? What did he feel?

Just because she'd lost her mind, didn't mean he had. Just because he met her halfway in her dreams didn't mean he would when he was released from medical and cleared to return to duty.

Duty.

What did duty dictate for either of them?

She wasn't new to fear. Fear had sent them into their long sleep. But this fear, which was obviously less life threatening, felt worse than that fear.

Why?

Tim lifted a towel to his glistening face and rubbed it, his body turning in her direction. She stepped back quickly, then slipped away, afraid of what she'd see in his eyes when he saw her.

And afraid of what she wouldn't see.

———

"We have a problem," Delilah "Doc" Clementyne avoided looking at General Halliwell as she began the process of delivering this new round of bad news. She couldn't even play the good news, bad news card. So far, there was no good news card in her deck.

In the wall's reflection, she saw him turn around. And she heard his sigh.

"What now?"

"Do you remember that geologist the Garradians borrowed?"

There was a short silence. He was pretending to think, but she knew he didn't need to. He had every person's name they'd loaned to the Garradians on mental speed dial.

"Dr. Walker." Another pause. "Dr. Miles Walker. What did he do? Oh wait. Let me guess. He made first contact."

"It was probably a given," Doc said. It was an unexpected that she'd pretty much expected. So technically, not unexpected. "There seems to be a woman in the mix."

She knew the general wanted to rant about it, but it was difficult for him. He'd gone on a mission and come back involved with an alien. It was also almost a given that anyone who went out on an expedition came back in love with an alien.

She cast a quick glance at her alien. Hel grinned.

None of them had a leg to stand on.

"Do we have a solution?" Halliwell asked.

"Well, we have to form a mission to try to contain the fall-out. The Maestra has suggested Riina Katala and Tim." Doc once again kept her tone carefully neutral.

Dr. Miles Walker was one of theirs and neither Riina or Tim were part of the Expedition. But they had done a mission with the General. He knew them both very well and respected them.

Now the General did look around. Doc warily turned to face him.

"Is Tim out of medical?"

"Yes, and he is finishing up his physical therapy." Tim, a former robot with a human consciousness, had recently transferred that consciousness back into a body cloned from his own DNA.

She had to give their ship's captain, CabeX, kudos for forward thinking. Back when the robots had left their human bodies, he'd foreseen a time when they might want to go back to their original forms and saved their DNA.

Not all of them had ended up back in their own cloned bodies, however. Necessity had required different outcomes for some of them. But Tim was back in a version of his own body.

That should have meant an easy integration, but apparently living for years in a robot body required a lot of adjustment when leaving the big, bad robot body behind.

She wasn't unsympathetic. She'd had to make some big adjustments since coming to the Garradian Galaxy—the biggest one being Helfron Giddioni.

She might still be trying to get used to his name. And having an alien and hostile mother-in-law. And becoming a step-mom to two little Giddionis. And…the nanites living inside her… well, a lot of adjustments to new things.

Hel's lips quirked up as if he knew what she was thinking. He probably did. They were connected in ways that was yet another of those adjustments.

"Other than Dr. Miles being our guy, what does this have to do with me?" Halliwell rubbed his face.

"The Maestra wanted you to be informed, in case you wanted to embed one of your people in the mission."

The general sighed again. "I, yes, I do. Let me think about who to send." He glanced up in time to catch her slight grimace. "Not a diplomat."

Yes, they both still had issues with diplomats.

"Thank you, sir." She knew how to look demure when needed and she deployed the look now.

The general snorted. "Dismissed, Doc."

"Yes, sir."

It wasn't an oversight that he never acknowledged Hel unless forced to by circumstances. The general knew how to hold a grudge.

Hel waited until they were safely outside to laugh.

"Do you think he'll task himself…" Hel began.

"No, he won't," Doc told him. "He'll want to, but he won't."

She meshed her fingers with his and saw the heat spark in his eyes. The general and his issues faded from her mind. And Doc was pretty sure they faded from Hel's too.

————

Tim followed CabeX into the meeting room. Trac—TrackerY— came in last and stopped near the door. The robotic cyborg couldn't show unease, but Tim knew Trac well enough to know how much Trac didn't want to be in this room with them.

Tim hadn't asked CabeX why he'd detailed Trac to the mission—partly because Tim didn't know what the mission was. And CabeX always had his reasons for what he did. His crew had learned to just follow orders.

The Garradian Maestra was already in the room. It was not a surprise to see Moose—also a former cyborg—at her back, since they were a couple.

She smiled a greeting, then gave CabeX a puzzled look.

"I don't believe I've met…" she didn't finish the sentence, just indicated Trac with a wave of her hand.

It was true that as cybernetic robots, the *Najer* crew weren't that different in appearance—to others—at first. But each of them had been specific models with special functions, over and above their basic intimidation factors. And as these people came to know them, they'd gradually been able to discern the differences in their various models.

And now only two of them remained in robot form, so it should be a lot easier. But it was also true that Trac didn't get out a lot. Tim wasn't sure he'd been off the ship at all since they started working with the Expedition and the Garradians.

"This is TrackerY," CabeX said. "Trac," he added.

"Trac. Pleased to meet you." She still looked puzzled.

Trac inclined his head, his hands folded across his massive, metal chest.

"Ma'am," he said. His voice was the most robotic of the crew's.

Tim had always figured it was a personal choice.

"He doesn't leave the *Najer* that often," CabeX said.

"Okay." The Maestra blinked a couple of times, gave a slight head shake, then gestured for them to take seats.

All of them but Trac did. He stayed near the door as the Maestra began to explain the problem unfolding on Arroxan Prime.

Tim might be surprised he was being tasked with the mission. It sounded like a diplomatic problem. None of the crew off the *Najer* were particularly good at that. Breaking things. Shooting things. Hacking into things. Yes. Talking nice? No.

"Who else is on the mission?" Tim finally asked. Surely someone from the Earth Expedition was going, since it was their guy in trouble. Or possibly in trouble. They didn't seem quite sure about that yet.

A list appeared on a screen in front of them. The only name Tim saw was Riina Katala. His newly human body reacted strongly, his heartbeat speeding up. And other parts felt strange and alien. *Riina.*

He hadn't seen her since he'd gone into medical for his consciousness transfer. He'd half hoped she'd come to see him, been mostly relieved she hadn't. He hadn't liked feeling so much less as he fought to recover from the transfer and accustom himself to a mostly human body.

He didn't know how to feel or act around her from inside this body.

He might be glad the choice had been removed. Now he'd have to see her.

"I'm conflicted about sending one person so obviously alien," the Maestra admitted, her glance flicking to Tim.

He did have obvious cybernetics. Like some of the others, he'd been reluctant to completely live without cybernetics.

"They don't have…" CabeX stopped as if unsure how to phrase the question.

Tim couldn't help him out.

"From what we can tell, no, but we're going in as alien anyway. And there is a bigger problem than just accidental first contact," she admitted.

A report popped up on his personal screen. It took him longer to absorb it than he was used to, but he still looked up before CabeX.

CabeX had gone fully human.

"Interesting," he said.

"Can I bring my my Skitterfin?" Trac asked. "My pet."

They all turned to look at him.

Trac had a pet?

Tim looked at CabeX who gave a shrug.

"Sure."

CabeX didn't sound sure, but if it got Trac out and about…

"Sure," Tim echoed. What was a skitterfin?

2

"Our passengers are entering the flight deck, Captain."

Captain Nevv Kellen looked up from his control deck. Veirn, the *Quendala's* onboard AI, was broadcasting video from the flight deck.

Kellen had studied their information packets, supplied to him by the Maestra, but this was his first time getting eyes on some of them. He'd flown missions with Riina and Tim before, though this was a new Tim, a mostly human Tim. Or somewhat human Tim? Only time would answer that question.

The TrackerY robot, Trac, was a disturbing sight with the three-tailed skitterfin on his shoulder. Its three tails wrapped his cyborg head and its wings were tucked in.

Nevv had never liked skitterfens. As a general rule he didn't like any animals on his ship. They were difficult to control and often acted on impulse. Its inclusion in the mission had been done without his input.

He studied the female soldier walking behind Trac. Her name was Lt. Lovely Dish, so he'd expected her to be anything but lovely. He wasn't sorry to be wrong.

He'd noticed when anyone mentioned Lieutenant Dish, the men fell silent. Now he knew why.

She was blonde, generously built, and her walk might have stalled his thinking for several seconds. Or longer.

It was a small team, but Arroxan Prime wasn't a high priority contact planet, being situated off the beaten flight paths and isolated in their little system. He'd studied the system, too, and had mentally labeled it as mostly dysfunctional. It had only one slightly habitable planet. How had anyone found their way there?

They were only sending the mission because contact had happened, not because any of them wanted to make contact with the planet's inhabitants.

From his perusal of the mission report, Dr. Miles Walker had gone to investigate a seismic warning sensor and tripped over everything in sight. And several things not in sight.

At least he seemed to realize it. He'd been deployed with a robot assist module named Harold—there had to be a story there—but even it couldn't save Dr. Walker from himself. Or from first contact.

On the good news side of the equation, the contact was limited so far. Nothing official yet.

They'd have probably just pulled Dr. Walker and Harold out, but the problem that had triggered the sensor seemed to be systemic and possibly planet-wide.

Current protocol was to interfere as little as possible in a planet's affairs, but back before the long sleep? A lot of interfering had occurred, with Arroxan Prime as a, well, prime example. He wasn't clear on the nature of the interference, but if sensors had been planted? Interfering had occurred.

There was a short delay at the boarding ramp, as man and robot signaled for the two women to board first. Riina didn't hesitate, but Lt. Dish engaged in a short argument with Tim before giving in and coming aboard.

With some reluctance, he stood, smoothing down his uniform before turning and striding to the hatch. It was time to welcome the team aboard.

———

Riina led the way to the *Quendala's* lounge. Even if she hadn't been aboard this ship before, its design was similar to others of its type that had been brought back into service as more and more of them woke from the long sleep. It helped to lead their small group. This meant she didn't have to look at Tim yet. They'd exchanged greetings at the hatch, of course, but somehow their glances hadn't intersected.

As she walked down the main corridor, she tried to ignore the tingling sensations traveling up and down her back. It was probably her imagination that Tim stared at her. That and wishful thinking? She pushed that thought away as firmly as she could manage.

From the opposite direction, the captain, Nevv Kellen approached, lifting a hand in greeting.

She was pleased to be traveling with him once more. He had a steady head in a crisis and was also brave and resourceful. The ship's AI, Veirn, had an interesting sense of humor, but personality quirks seemed to be the order of the day as more and more of the Garradian assets were assembled and reactivated.

"Captain," she said, giving him a respectful nod, before smiling and holding out her hand.

He took her hand, but his attention shifted past her. Either to Lt. Dish or the team in general, she wasn't sure. Well, she might suspect it was Lt. Dish. She seemed to have an interesting effect on the men.

"Small team this time," Kellen noted. "Optimism or…"

"Caution," Riina finished. They weren't exactly expecting

things to go badly, but Arroxan Prime was a planet that did not appear to have indulged in any type of star ward looking. And, between experience and time spent in Doc's company, Riina was learning to expect the unexpected. And the worst from the unexpected.

It was entirely possible the populace would become a little agitated at the realization that first contact had happened. Or a lot. Full on panic was also on what Doc liked to call the Bingo card, whatever that meant. And they might reject any attempts to help them with their Vorthari infestation.

There was the video from Dr. Walker's contact, but would they believe it? The Vorthari were unusual appearing aliens. Unsettling but also beautiful. The aliens, the Skaridrex, who'd helped contain the Vorthari at the initial contact site were not beautiful. That might be a problem.

Multiple Garradian scientific teams had studied the data transmitted from Dr. Walker's encounter with the Vorthari. They hoped to discover their origins and why they'd migrated to Arroxan Prime. They were all certain they weren't natural to the planet. She wasn't sure why yet.

There was one theory currently being discussed that the Vorthari were the source of the extreme volcanic activity the planet experienced. Did that mean the Vorthari predated the human occupants?

Anything was possible which was just another way of saying, "expect the unexpected."

"We have contact with Dr. Walker and Harold," Riina continued. So far everything he'd supplied indicated a people who weren't that interested in the stars. Even their alien conspiracy theories seemed to be focused underground.

And they weren't wrong about that.

There was a short pause, then the captain cleared his throat.

"You'll each find a path customized to your ID that will lead you to your quarters. We'll be lifting off shortly. Locate your secure seating for both lift-off and when we activate the star drive or you'll have some unpleasant moments."

They had to be well clear of the outpost before they could activate the star drive, Riina knew.

"Thank you, Captain," Riina said. She glanced at her time-piece. "Let's return here in half an hour? We have some video from Dr. Walker to study. It's from their entertainment broadcasts. We need to get a feel for the inhabitants of Arroxan Prime."

"Cool," Lt. Dish said. She bent to pick up her gear, but Trac beat her—and Tim—to it.

"Let me assist you," Trac said. "I have no gear to stow."

Now Tim turned toward her, but it felt as if he avoided her gaze.

"You brought no gear?" he asked.

"I brought it aboard earlier," Riina said. She and the captain had needed to discuss their approach to the planet.

Was it her imagination that Tim's gaze shot toward the captain for a few seconds?

She gave an imperceptible sigh. This mission was going to be challenging on multiple levels.

3

Pollin Sollin walked quickly down the quiet street, stopping at intervals to check his surroundings. And once he stopped for a particularly troublesome tremor. Their leaders claimed the seismic activity wasn't getting worse, but Pollin wasn't sure he believed them.

He stopped in front of a two-story house—none of their buildings were particularly tall—glanced both ways and then slipped up to the door, using the shadows of the low-lying bushes in the yard as much as possible.

He gave the knock. Listened for the return knock. Knocked again.

The door opened just enough for him to slip inside. A blanket hung over the door, so that no light could escape into the street. The windows had been blacked out, too.

Despite these precautions, the lighting was dim, the shapes around the room shadowy.

Any other night, the precautions would have amused him.

He knew everyone there. And they knew him. There'd been no new members since Herk Taan had relocated to the southern pole.

He had been a good recruiter, too good some thought.

It wasn't that their gathering was illegal. Their government was indifferent to their cause. But sometimes employers were less willing to overlook their level of interest in alien life forms.

"Has anyone heard from Herk?" Drun Marik was their unofficial head. He had to be particularly careful because he worked for state security.

His bosses probably knew what Drun got up to in his spare time, but he was good at his job and what was the harm?

Pollin took an empty seat at the back. He wasn't sure, but he thought he was the last one there. He'd debated coming. He sat with his hands clenched in his lap, his fist clenching and unclenching.

At first, he'd been so excited. This was what they'd been waiting for, searching for, planning for.

But was *this* that?

He touched the data sheet tucked in his jacket's inside pocket.

Two signals. He'd identified two signals. He'd confirmed two signals.

One planet based.

And one space based.

He wasn't wrong.

He wanted to be wrong.

Only he wasn't.

It wasn't as if signals of this type could be faked.

He was almost one hundred percent sure they couldn't be faked.

He knew one person who would know if Pollin had stumbled into something governmental, something that would be illegal to know about.

Drun would know. But if he knew, why hadn't he said something or at least hinted at it?

Was it because one of the signals was space based? Had the government finally turned their attention to the stars?

There were so few of them who looked up, even in their group. From the time they learned to walk, his people looked down. It was the only way to keep from falling when a tremor hit.

If one was star gazing, one would soon be face planting.

"Any new business?" Drun asked.

Pollin realized he'd missed all the old business while lost in his thoughts. He took a steadying breath. It was now or never.

He lifted his hand, glad the light was too bad for anyone to see the tremble. Then he rose.

"I have," he hesitated, not sure what to call it, "information."

4

Tim wished he could miss the meeting. Gathering? Consultation? But he was, he'd been informed, co-team leader with Riina.

It was as if they'd set out to torture him.

She'd avoided him since he became human again.

And now that he was human, he could see, could even *sense* when other males were interested in Riina on a more personal level.

These moments of knowing were distracting, painful even. He'd taken to staring at himself in the mirror, trying to get his expression under control before interacting with humans. With Riina.

He probably didn't need to, since she wouldn't look at him. Was she so disgusted by his human body?

He'd known when he decided to use his own DNA, to become himself again, that there was risk. For one thing, he'd forgotten what he'd looked like before. And for another, his human form could have been unappealing to humans not of his race. Or of his race, if he ever found any of them.

He could have picked a Garradian clone. They all seemed to

be attractive. But he'd wanted to be himself again. It was going to be hard enough to be human without the extra difficulty of an unfamiliar body.

So, what had seemed like a good reason to become himself again had turned out to be less so. For instance, his consciousness appeared to have forgotten all about who and what he'd been. First thing he'd done was fall on his face.

He and his body were doing better, well enough for the mission. But the fit still felt awkward and unfamiliar.

They'd probably sent Trac along to look out for him. Because Trac didn't want to go anywhere, and he really didn't want to go anywhere not in the *Najer*. And yet here he was.

A bodyguard. Him. He'd been one of the toughest of the robotic models. And now he had a babysitter.

He hesitated outside the hatch, pulling his thoughts in and, hopefully, schooling his expression. This had been so much easier when he hadn't had an expression.

He activated the hatch in time to hear Riina say, "At least only two inhabitants of Arroxan Prime know that first contact has been made. That should make our job easier."

Tim heard a gentle cough behind him and turned to find Lt. Dish standing behind him holding a bowl filled with white... something. Something that smelled delicious. This was one part of being human he did not mind. Delicious things were so... delicious.

"I brought popcorn for the movie," she said.

5

"It might," Drun Marik said, "have been better if you'd brought this straight to me."

"It's against our charter," Pollin said. Not that he didn't agree with Drun. They'd had to step out into the rear of the building to hear themselves think over the sounds coming from the meeting room.

"Yes." Drun sighed. "Well, it's done now." He paced away, then back. "You're sure?"

Pollin knew that Drun asked the question, not because he didn't believe Pollin, but because he wanted him to be wrong. It was a false hope.

"What troubles me," Pollin said, "well, what troubles me the most, who are these aliens in contact with here on Arroxan Prime?"

He didn't use the word traitor, not yet. Whoever it was might not be a traitor. They could be a fool.

"Can you track that signal back to its source?" Drun asked. "We could check them out before we go...official."

Official. It had been done. Once or twice. It never went

well. Again, it wasn't that their government was particularly oppressive. It was more like impatient with anything that didn't directly relate to fixing their tremor problems.

And it always impacted employment. One got an unstable tag added to their name and it was good-bye paycheck.

"I already did that," Pollin admitted. "I have the location here." He patted his breast pocket.

"Do you have a name to go with the location?"

Pollin could tell Drun sensed another level of reluctance from him.

"It's…" he had to pause to take a breath that wasn't panicked, "Lira Taan."

Drun inhaled sharply. "Lira. But…she's an archaeologist."

"It didn't make sense to me either unless," he hesitated, "I haven't heard from Herk, but I did find some new data from the southern pole. Troubling data." He turned to face Drun. "He might be dead. The facility is gone."

"Gone." Drun repeated the word as if it would somehow help.

Pollin took out a small hand-held, activated it and then searched for several minutes, before handing it to Drun.

Drun studied the overflight photos that Pollin had managed to get without alerting anyone. It wasn't as if seismic activity was unusual anywhere on Arroxan Prime.

Drun studied the image, zoomed in on the location. Zoomed out. Zoomed in again.

"It's…gone." He looked at Pollin. "What about the seismic? Can we get that without…"

"I know someone. I should have it by tomorrow." Pollin bit his lip for several seconds. "Do you think its related to…"

He didn't finish the question. He didn't need to. Drun knew what he meant.

"We need to talk to Lira. Unofficially," Drun said, with emphasis.

She was the daughter of a friend. They owed her that.

"Do we…"

Drun cut him off. "We don't warn her. We can't, Pollin, not even for Herk's sake."

6

Tim wasn't used to having expectations. According to his other ship mates, it took training to learn to have expectations, and then more training on how to tailor them to reality.

That seemed like an almost circular problem that could better be avoided by not having expectations, trained or otherwise. He thought he had the whole concept handled.

It was a shock to find out he was wrong.

He'd hoped—half expected—the transit to Arroxan Prime to include opportunities to get back onto a better footing with Riina. That she'd have time to get comfortable with his human form. And that he'd get more comfortable with it.

So far, it wasn't working.

He couldn't blame it on too many people around. The ship was barely manned, though technically it didn't need any humans since the ship's AI Veirn could handle most anything that came along.

In practice, what this meant was that the humans—and Trac—had too much time on their hands. This resulted in multiple awkward encounters, interrupted opportunities, and too much time to think.

His human brain thought *way* too much. And most of the thinking wasn't productive in any way that he could identify.

They'd gone over the possible mission parameters so many times, even Lt. Dish could recite them from memory.

It wasn't, he realized, kind to conclude that Lt. Dish wasn't as smart as the rest of them. He knew this logically. He had no idea why he'd made the assumption that she was less smart. Perhaps it was because she brought popcorn to their strategy meetings?

He was aware that by human standards, or rather by Expedition standards, she was remarkably attractive. He'd noted that male heads swiveled in her direction when they'd make their way toward the ship.

Before they'd left, he'd downloaded some data on Earth attraction metrics and applied them to Lt. Dish. She'd scored very high.

Next, he'd assessed his own physical response to being in her presence. He had noted some elevated readings, but none that were as high as when he was around Riina. From that he concluded that he found her attractive, but in a detached way.

Had that detachment led him to conclude she was less intelligent than he was?

It was possible. He wasn't sure why she'd been included in the mission at all.

She was a lieutenant. This put her fairly low on the rank structure within the Expedition.

Rank didn't matter that much on the ship, since none of them were in that rank structure, so perhaps the general had considered any rank sufficient. But to what end? She couldn't order any of them around.

Conclusion: she must have some other purpose.

Before becoming human, he would have asked Riina for her assessment of Lt. Dish.

Now his issues felt compounded by the distance, and by

what he'd observed as her reaction to the lieutenant. He could be wrong, but he sensed a faint, deeply buried hostility from Riina.

What was that about?

Other than providing popcorn, Lt. Dish didn't talk much, didn't appear to observe much, and contributed zero to their discussions.

She looked good. And she looked.

That seemed to be the sum of Lt. Dish.

And yes, as she moved around, even Tim, who prided himself on not noticing human emotions, sensed waves of something swirling around her.

She was, he decided, a disruptor of some kind. Was that her function?

They were getting closer to Arroxan Prime. If he didn't do something, they'd arrive and things and people would still be confusing.

He needed to talk to someone. He wanted that someone to be Riina.

He went back to the Earth data he'd downloaded. Surely there was something in there about how to talk to a woman who used to be your friend and was now giving off strange vibes?

―――――

This wasn't the first time the team had viewed the data that Dr. Walker had sent from Arroxan Prime. Rinna wondered if everyone else was as confused as she was. It didn't help reminding herself she wasn't a geologist. She was an astrophysicist. And a scientist. That should help with comprehension.

Only it didn't.

"If we can solve the problem planet-wide, it might be possible for us to get in and get out without widening our first contact exposure," she said, into the silence that had followed the viewing.

"Are we sure we've received all the data available?" Veirn asked the question, its voice coming from the speaker system.

Shouldn't Veirn know the answer to that question? Rinna frowned.

"Are you showing gaps in the data, Veirn?" she asked.

"It is possible that gaps occurred while Dr. Walker's suit was recording events," the AI said, rather than giving a direct answer.

"I'm having a little trouble with the geology," Riina confessed.

"There's a lot of anomalous data," Lt. Dish said.

They all turned to look at her. This was the first time she'd done more than supply snacks to eat during the viewings.

"Anomalous?" Tim asked the question, which was a relief.

Riina was tired of being the only one who wasn't sure what was going on.

"Well, Dr. Walker himself makes several comments about the geology on Arroxan Prime being different from Earth geology. He doesn't seem to be sure what he's seeing and experiencing."

"You are familiar with Earth geology?" Riina asked.

Lt. Dish blinked a couple of times and then nodded. Riina had the sense that the lieutenant was surprised Riina didn't know this.

"It wasn't in the file I received from the general," Riina said, trying not to sound defensive. She already had, she'd had to face, issues with the young woman. She was so…lovely. It shouldn't be annoying that even the robot, Trac, tended to watch her when she was in the room. Certainly, the captain and Tim also appeared to have trouble keeping their eyes off her.

She knew from something she'd overheard that "dish" was

an Earth term for very nice looking, and that the Lieutenant was appropriately named. *Lovely Dish.*

"It's like her parents knew, even when she was a baby," one Earth woman had said. "If she wasn't so nice, I'd hate her, but you can't."

"No," her companion had said, followed by a sigh that seemed to Riina to indicate regret.

They wanted to hate her but couldn't. There seemed to be more there to understand about Earth culture, but over the few days of their journey, Riina did get the part of wanting to hate Lt. Dish. And not quite managing it. She found it much harder to like her.

"Interesting," Lt. Dish said, her head tipped to one side so that strands of her blonde hair dangled against the perfect curve of her cheek.

It took a moment for Riina to connect the lieutenant's statement with hers. Right. It was interesting that General Halliwell hadn't fully disclosed Lt. Dish's credentials.

"Can you think of a reason why the general didn't want us to know you had geologic knowledge?

"No." Lt. Dish shook her head, making random strands of her hair appear to dance.

It was really annoying. And kind of endearing, but mostly annoying.

No, what was really annoying was the look in Tim and the captain's eyes as they watched Lt. Dish.

She wanted to blame Lt. Dish for the reason they weren't making much progress in figuring out just what had happened during Dr. Walker's time beneath the surface of Arroxan Prime, but the captain had no reason to know any of this stuff.

And Tim? As a robot, he might have been able to efficiently process Dr. Walker's data, but she knew that his return to human form had significantly slowed his processing capacity.

She just hoped Lt. Dish wasn't scrambling what circuits he had left.

That thought put some heat into her cheeks and she turned from them to study the screen. She had no right to be upset by anything Tim did or thought or felt. They were *friends*. Or at least, she hoped they were still friends. Right now, it felt like they were polite strangers.

Every morning, after another night of tossing and turning with dreams where Tim played a prominent role, she'd have to spend time to get her expression and her feelings back into rigorous control. She liked to think that she'd seen some signs that Tim wanted to close that gap, to be friends again, but it seemed like something—or someone—always interrupted them when they might have been able to talk.

She wanted to lean against something and close her eyes. Instead, she stiffened her spine and stared at the last frozen image on the screen.

"Are we quite sure the Skaridrex are the good aliens?" The Vorthari were quite beautiful. It had been easy to be with Dr. Walker as he was trying to save them. Until it all went wrong and the Vorthari tried to kill him and his illegal, first contact friend.

Everyone wanted to be annoyed with Dr. Walker for that first contact, but everyone who could be mad at him hadn't a leg to stand on. Some had also made illegal or inadvertent first contact. Some had made inevitable first contact.

A bunch of them had fallen in love.

But none of those romances had threatened the survival of an entire planet. Was that a fair assessment? Probably not. Dr. Walker had uncovered an entire planet at risk. The question was, had he somehow given the Vorthari information to help them break free from their underground existence?

Even he didn't seem to know.

"There are, or there were," Veirn said, "nanites present.

When we are there, I should be able to connect with them and collect better data. Assuming they weren't damaged in the process."

"I wish we could access it now," Riina said. "I feel like we're flying into the unknown."

"Most flying," Tim said, "is into the unknown. Even when we knew, we didn't know enough. So still unknown."

Somehow their gazes met and held. It was the first time since his transition.

"At least," Tim qualified, "that has been my experience."

Her lips quirked up at the edges. "It has become my experience since…" She didn't finish the sentence. Everyone here knew she'd been wakened from a long sleep to a new, puzzling, and sometimes dangerous reality.

What surprised her now was that this moment, with Tim's gaze holding hers, felt more dangerous than anything she'd done since waking.

7

"Veirn," Captain Kellen said, "could you inform the crew that we'll be exiting star drive for the final time and should make orbit in two ship's increments. Convert those time stamps for the Earth crew, please."

Of course, the only Earth crew was Lt. Dish. Did Veirn need to convert for Tim or Trac? No, he decided. They could do their own conversions. But Lt. Dish—his thoughts did a weird kind of splutter that had only begun since she came on board.

"Roger that, Captain," Veirn said.

Kellen accepted the Earth acknowledgment without reaction. He was getting used to it, though he didn't understand how it had managed to filter into every AI he'd encountered since he woke. And it wasn't as if it was the only strangeness he'd had to deal with in this unexpected future.

Only Riina Katala knew that this transit had taken longer than it should have, despite the use of the star drive, because he'd also been tasked with making strategic stops to get updated survey information on the regions between Central Command and Arroxan Prime.

During their long sleep, some of their outposts had experienced minimal to catastrophic damage. None of it was a surprise, but it had left gaps in their knowledge base. This had been a good opportunity to fill some of those gaps. They'd initiated scans and dropped drones that could connect to the nearest working outpost to monitor the various systems.

None of the other passengers had appeared to notice their jump/pause transit, or if they had, they hadn't commented on it in his hearing. He'd enjoyed the feeling of actually transiting systems, rather than just passing through them in the quickest possible time.

He had chosen to become a ship's captain for a reason, that reason being that he liked exploring space. The short missions he'd been sent on since he woke had not nearly satisfied that desire.

There was a sound and a screen appeared on his console. Lt. Dish stood outside the bridge hatch, requesting permission to enter.

He ignored the sudden splutter of his thoughts and opened the hatch for her.

The Garradians had always had varying degrees of physical attractiveness, but it had never been a priority in creating couples. Competence was much more highly prized in his culture.

Perhaps, he thought, as he turned to watch Lt. Dish walk onto the bridge, they'd missed out on something.

Her uniform wasn't excessively tight, but it did fit her admirably shaped form. Everything about her was neat, contained, crisp and yet—there was a quality about her that was very far from crisp. She moved briskly and stopped to salute him, then lowered her arm and gave him a rueful look that almost stopped his heart.

"Do your people salute, Captain? I don't wish to offend."

"It's fine," Kellen said, fighting the urge to run a finger around his uniform collar. "Please, sit." He indicated the second-in-command position. He hadn't had a full crew complement since before the long sleep. Even at the rate they were waking up their people, they didn't have enough people to man a ship as they had in the past.

And they weren't waking up ship's crew. Their priority was scientists and other specialists who could help them rebuild their infrastructure. And that had been delayed when they'd had to respond to threats. He couldn't blame all of them on the Earth Expedition or the robot crew, but they had definitely played a part in arriving in the Garradian system trailing clouds of enemies.

Lt. Dish sat in the second chair, giving a little wriggle that he took to be delight. He arched a brow, and she gave him a rueful look.

"I grew up with *Star Trek*. It's like a dream come true to sit on the bridge of a spaceship," she explained. Perhaps something in his face prompted her to add, "I promise I won't touch anything."

She didn't know it, but she already touched "something." There were controls embedded in the arm rests she gripped, but they weren't active and wouldn't become active for her without some kind of triggering control. Such as the sudden extinction of the captain.

It was his turn to sense his expression turning wry.

"What can I do for you, Lieutenant?" It seemed wise to alter the subject before he embarrassed himself.

"I know we're dropping out of star drive soon," this also seemed to please her because her eyes gleamed with excitement, "but I was wondering how close to Arroxan Prime we'll be at that point."

Kellen activated a map of the Arroxan Prime star system—

one updated with data from the ship that had dropped Dr. Walker off—and added a data point for their arrival.

"I don't want to drop in too close to the planet. Star drive is not kind to large, solid objects," he added. It pleased him when she grinned, as if she understood the small joke. "And we want to do new data scans. Make sure nothing has changed and to restore comms with Dr. Walker."

Now Lt. Dish frowned. "Did we lose comms because of the star drive?"

Kellen hesitated. "It is possible. The systems we have transited are…complicated." He wasn't a scientist, but he'd learned enough to know complicated when he saw it. "And we dropped out of star drive several times."

He waited for her to ask, but she didn't. She just nodded.

"Why do you ask?"

"I've been studying the pattern of Dr. Walker's transmissions." She sighed and frowned. "I'm no expert on space transmissions, but it looks to me like his last transmission wasn't complete. As if there is data missing."

Kellen nodded. "It is possible our own transits cut off the data stream…"

He knew Veirn was listening and was probably already looking into it.

And then Veirn weighed in to the discussion. "Dr. Walker mentioned concern that someone planet-side might be tracking their transmissions."

"But," Lt. Dish's frown deepened, "according to him they lack the technology to disrupt…" Her voice trailed off. "Miss Marple."

"Excuse me?" Kellen said.

"She's an imaginary detective on Earth, but she always says don't believe what you're told."

"It is true that Dr. Walker couldn't know if the government had the ability to block his comms," Veirn said.

"So, it is possible that someone else down there knows we're coming?" Kellen didn't like that idea.

"I don't think they could—unless they could read the transmissions and that would take time," Lt. Dish pointed out.

"Cracking an alien language is most difficult," Veirn said.

And Veirn would know. It and its AI kin did it fairly regularly.

"They might not need to know what we're saying. Just the fact of the transmissions might cause…distress," Lt. Dish pointed out. "It's probably a good idea we're coming in kind of slow and easy."

"Yes," Kellen said. And they could also come in cloaked. That seemed an even better idea.

———

Now the bridge felt oddly full to Kellen. Riina and Tim were seated at the science station to his right. Trac, as was typical for the robot, stood in the corner, with his skitterfin wrapped around his neck. He didn't know how he could stand it. Of course, he was a cyborg. A robot. He couldn't feel it.

Lt. Dish was back in the number two seat at his left.

Four bodies total and it felt crowded. He wondered what Veirn thought of the sudden intrusion into what had been their space alone? Could an AI care?

"Dropping out of star drive in five…four…three…two…one…"

Star drive transitions were advertised as smooth by the scientists who'd created them, but they'd oversold smooth a little. And Kellen now knew that what space one dropped into also played a part.

This transition was bumpy, but it didn't seem to affect Trac. The robot rode the bumpy slowing as if it were nonexistent.

Kellen was glad he was strapped in. And that he'd insisted the others strap in.

The other feature of the transition into normal space was the lag while the sensors came back online and began delivering data. Near space was easier. Far space took longer for all the obvious reasons, the main one being it was further away.

While he waited for sensors to begin delivering, he pulled up the data from Dr. Walker's drop-off ship. It had also noticed unusual bumpiness and disruptions in the data. It was yet another reason, in his opinion, on why no one had visited the system much. But it didn't explain how a human civilization had managed to develop here.

The original data from before the sleep offered no explanation for Arroxan Prime or why or how it had come to the attention of their scientists. It was an uncomfortable mystery, even for an explorer of space and one much used to the puzzling.

"We are starting to receive data," Veirn said.

Forward screens flickered to life and planetary objects began to appear.

Riina released her restraints and stood up, pacing forward until she stopped next to him.

"Any sign of a transmission from Dr. Walker?" she asked.

"No."

Did Veirn sound concerned by that? It was hard for Kellen to tell when the AI felt emotion. If the AI felt emotion?

"What kind of inter-system interference are you detecting?" Riina asked.

"Quite a bit," Veirn said. "Most of the outgoing transmissions we have already picked up."

"Let's begin transmitting to Dr. Walker…" Kellen said.

"I would recommend waiting on that, Captain," Veirn said. "Until we get closer and the data is more definitive."

Kellen looked at Riina and saw concern in her eyes that probably echoed the look in his. They hadn't been out of contact for that long, but even when factoring in the distances in space, events could change rapidly and in unexpected ways.

"We'll hold any transmissions," Kellen said, he glanced back. "And we are going in cloaked."

"I was going to suggest that," Riina said. "The longer we can postpone detection from any possible observers, the better."

8

Dr. Miles Walker was unhappy with the location that had been sent to him for the rendezvous. If he'd been able to, he'd have told them that he and Lira and her father had barely escaped alive from a site with *less* seismic activity than where they were currently standing. He closed it again. Everyone present thought Harold was the alien from outer space. Miles had managed to escape detection so far by looking like an innocuous human. Admitting that he'd been present at the disaster at the planet's southern pole? Not a good idea.

He should spend the time coming up with an explanation for why there was a crowd here. Okay, it wasn't technically a crowd. Ten people max were milling around. They'd arrived separately, covertly he'd have called it. They were clumped together in small groups, talking excitedly in low voices.

But it was way more than the three that the incoming team would be expecting.

These were, according to Lira, the members of her father's alien watchers club. They might not call themselves that. They probably had a more scientific name for it because using science made it all sound less crazy.

Only it wasn't crazy anymore.

They were here to meet the aliens who could be arriving at any moment. The aliens they *knew* were incoming.

Once Harold had told him their comms were actually being tracked by this group of conspiracy theorists, they'd had to stop communicating with the incoming *Quendala*. Harold had managed to send a last warning, though it had lacked specificity. Such as, you're going to be met with a contingent of the planet's most wacky, but they are ridiculously excited to meet aliens, so it should all be good.

Miles eyed the man Lira had called Drun. Miles had a feeling he was the government plant in the group. Even the most extreme groups got a government plant back on Earth. It helped head off things like, well, this.

Only it hadn't headed it off.

Miles glanced around. At least, not yet. They could be out there, too. Waiting and watching. And his people were flying right into it.

Harold stood in the center of the group, though no one stood near it. It was as if Harold were the bullseye in the center of the target. Miles shifted uneasily. He didn't like it, but if he edged up to Harold, he risked exposure, possibly arrest, and that alien autopsy he was hoping to avoid.

And—any action he took now also put Lira and her father at more risk. The group was already seriously unhappy with Lira's father for keeping all the alien goodness to himself.

He couldn't help recalling *Star Trek First Contact* ending when the alien ship arrived and the people were just standing around like it was not that big of a deal. Zefram Cochrane had been a little freaked out, and he'd known they were coming. Of course, Zefram had also known they were peaceful incoming aliens. This bunch didn't know that for sure.

It had been difficult to share too much information because he and Harold didn't know exactly who was coming. What if it was the intimidating Doc? No way he could make her less scary.

He glanced at Lira, noticed T'Korrin's beak just visible inside her suit. The cold was both bitter and intense and she was used to the bird riding inside her suit with her.

He'd almost suggested leaving T'Korrin behind, but he had managed to stop himself in time. He might be a dude, a geologist, and an alien, but he had heard about women and their pets. It made no sense to bring a pet into a possibly volatile situation, but it wasn't his call to make, not if he wanted to ever kiss the girl again.

There was a murmur through the group—again, not a crowd—as a bright light burst into view in the sky. One of the group held some kind of tracking handheld and was studying it, then looking up and pointing.

So, they were here.

He looked at Lira. She looked at him. He wished they were anywhere else. Okay, not anywhere, but certainly somewhere more stable and private. Definitely somewhere warmer.

As if the ground beneath them shared the group's growing excitement, tremors began to shudder through the icy surface.

It was geologically interesting that this location was also turbulent seismically. Miles was rather proud of the fact that he was able to ride the tremors like a native. He caught Lira giving him a quick smile before redirecting her attention toward the pinpoint of light that seemed to be closing in on their position.

Harold shifted from one foot to the other, distracting Miles from the sky view.

Shifting was never a good sign with the robot. What was the problem?

He felt his own feet shifting as he stopped himself from stepping up next to the robot.

Something was wrong. What could be wrong?

He was one hundred percent sure his people wouldn't start

firing on the waiting group. He wasn't so sure about the group. He had noticed they were all armed. For their peaceful meeting with aliens. Apparently hypocrisy wasn't just an Earth thing.

There was a sudden surge of light and then it was as if an ink bottle had been spilled in the sky. The dark mass spread quickly, shutting out the light from the stars and the southern moon. But the pinpoint of light continued to close on them. And then he realized it was hovering directly overhead.

Shouldn't it be bigger? And more ship shaped?

He angled his head right. Then he angled it left. There was no discernible ship in the inky mass. so how—and what—had closed in on them?

A light appeared to one side of the pinpoint light, still small. Then another and another until a pattern of lights were overhead.

Miles felt his unease spike.

"We need to move," he said, though hide is what he meant.

The pattern of lights grew brighter and then began to pulse.

"Move!" he yelled!

"Yes," Harold said. It began to move, slowly at first, then rapidly.

The group began to widen the circle but they weren't moving fast enough.

"We are peaceful people," one of the men said.

Miles thought his name was Pollin.

"Be peaceful from behind that snow pile!" Miles yelled as the bright lights began to change color and pulse faster.

The group still only widened the circle. Miles grabbed Lira's hand and pulled her behind a pile of ice boulders and then yanked her down next to him. He thought he heard T'Korrin squawk. Perhaps that sound encouraged the others to follow suit.

Just in time, the wide bare stretch of ice flow emptied.

Something began to heave up *from* the ice as light stabbed down from the ink blot.

Whatever it was coming out of the ice intersected with the incoming and was sucked into what looked like a dark funnel. Some of the sucking didn't go well as flying pieces of something began to splat onto the surface around them.

And on them.

Miles scrapped a piece off his forehead and looked at it.

"It's Vorthari," he told Lira. "At least, a piece of one."

"It was coming up," Lira said, her eyes wide in a suddenly pale face. "But how did they know?"

"I don't know," Miles said. He looked up. Who was up there? And where was the Garradian ship?

9

"Houston," Lt. Dish said, "I think we have a problem?"

"Excuse me?" Riina said.

Tim was happy Rinna had said it. Who was Houston?

"Sorry, it's an Earth thing. It means, well," Lt. Dish gave a shrug, "that we have a problem."

"A large problem," Trac said from his corner of the bridge. "What manner of entity is this?"

Captain Kellen had already slowed their forward momentum and altered their trajectory as soon as their sensors had flagged the unknown entity seeming to arrive just ahead of them.

Was it a ship? It didn't look like a ship, though for a brief instant, their sensors had caught a shape before it began to spread out.

Tim's ship, the *Najer*, had been a lot of places and they had observed a large quantity of ship types. There tended to be certain similarities among space going vessels. Similarities that fell into classes, such as shipping, battle, scout. Of course, each species' ships had peculiarities, but they still tended to look like, well, ships.

This, whatever it was, did not look like a ship or ships. He wasn't sure what it looked like.

"Blobs," Lt. Dish said. "Are we sure they are ships?"

"Miasma," Riina said. "It is oddly formed and indistinct. If we were to observe this…object…elsewhere, I would postulate that it might be a quasar, cosmic dust, a gravitational wave…it's too small to be a dark galaxy, but there are some indications…"

She stopped.

"It's almost bubble-like," Lt. Dish said. She too rose, as if sitting made it harder to think.

Tim unstrapped and rose, but he experienced no change in his lack of comprehension.

"It is blocking light from the planet," Tim said. Perhaps standing had helped? If his comment was helpful? He did know how planets that were inhabited tended to look from space. Large clusters of occupants created clusters of light that even showed through storm clouds. But darkness was slowly spreading across the surface of Arroxan Prime, blotting out all observable light.

"Tim's right," Riina said, flashing him a quick, anxious look. "The lights are going out. Or our ability to see them is being mitigated."

"I should go down," Trac said. The skitterfin wrapped around his neck lifted its head and looked at him with large, dark eyes.

His words also caused everyone on the bridge to turn and look at him. Tim felt a stab of something. If only he weren't in this human body. Though it wasn't completely human.

"We could go down," Tim said. He might have emphasized the "we."

"You would slow me down," Trac said. The skitterfin turned to stare at Tim. Did it agree with Trac?

No one could claim that Trac had been gifted with tact. Though to be fair, none of them had been gifted with that as robots. It wasn't standard in their programming. Only their lone human, Kraye, might have cause to complain about the lack, since he'd been the only one on board the *Najer* with feelings.

But he'd never said anything.

"I have enough cybernetics to be useful," Tim said.

Riina seemed to open her mouth, but then she pressed her lips together.

"No one should go down until we know more. Let's give the sensors time to collect data. Veirn, any early insights into what that is?"

"I do not believe it is natural," Veirn said. "There is evidence of propulsion."

One of the forward screens changed. It took Tim a couple of seconds to process this new data.

"It is an energy trail." The entity had arrived in the system from almost the opposite side they'd come in from. He started a search through the available Garradian data on what was beyond this system in that direction.

He had cause to know that space was wide, vast, and mysterious. But it was only since he'd become human that he'd processed that information as awe-inspiring and yes, overwhelming. His more finite brain struggled to grasp just how big, while his memories showed previous matter-of-fact acceptance.

The two realities sat uncomfortably together inside his mind.

"I should be on the team that goes to the surface," Lt. Dish said.

This statement had the benefit of redirecting all attention her way.

"Why…" Riina began. The captain made a sound that was clearly negative.

"Dr. Walker is my mission directive," she said. "I'm the lone Expedition representative. And I agree, we should get down there and find Dr. Walker and Harold."

If Dr. Walker was her mission imperative, then Harold was

most likely Tim's, since the robot was Garradian. Or did that make the robot the captain's imperative?

His human brain was once again experiencing dissonance.

They were still closing in on Arroxan Prime, though at a different angle, one that wouldn't put them in orbit, but rather send them on a close pass. Tim suspected that the captain planned to make a wide turn back, which would allow them to examine the other side of the planet and determine how widespread the intrusion was.

"Based on our last communication with Dr. Walker," Tim said, "our rendezvous coordinates were here."

He made those coordinates appear on the display that showed them the planet.

"If we dropped a stealth shuttle as we pass by, we should be able to reach those coordinates, collect the doctor, and rendezvous with the *Quendala* as it makes a wide loop back around."

"To wait until we've made a complete pass risks the loss of Dr. Walker and Harold," Trac agreed.

"Something disruptive is occurring on the planet surface," Veirn said. "We are receiving data that could indicate surface explosions."

"Explosions?" Riina's voice was sharp. "They have a lot of seismic disruptions…"

"These are not typical of the previously recorded seismic disruptions," Veirn actually interrupted her.

Tim blinked at this. It was most unusual.

"It is possible," Veirn continued, "that the alien anomaly we are observing is firing on the planet."

"We can't…" Riina began but was interrupted again. By Lt. Dish.

"We can't leave our people, our person or Harold down there," she said.

"But beyond that," Captain Kellen said, "if some entity is

attacking Arroxan Prime, it is our duty to discover why and how."

"And intervene?" Lt. Dish asked the question Tim was thinking.

Kellen hesitated. "I will send data back to Central Command, but it will take time to get a response back. In the meantime, all we can do is assess. We are only seeing one side of the situation."

"So, you concur that we need to send a team to the surface," Tim said.

Kellen hesitated, then nodded with clear reluctance. "If Dr. Walker weren't down there? I'd advise a wait and see for now, but…we need to ascertain his condition and situation."

"Hasn't he acquired a side chick?" Lt. Dish asked.

"A…" Riina looked at her.

"A girlfriend?" Lt. Dish prompted. "What about her?"

"It's not as if we haven't evacuated at risk individuals before," Riina said, "but I believe there is her father. And she has family. It could get complicated very quickly."

Tim found he could grin. "Because that's never happened before."

Riina looked at him with her eyes and smiled as they both remembered their mission with General Halliwell and how that had gone.

The moment of connection helped. For just that second, he felt they were friends again.

10

They'd had to move quickly. Their point-of-no-return was coming up faster than Riina liked.

The shuttle had been kitted out with first contact kits, both physical and as much data as the system had space for, but now they were adding weapons loadouts, which she didn't like at all, but accepted were necessary.

Captain Kellen seemed resigned to being left alone on the *Quendala*, though Riina had the sense he wished he could come with them.

Veirn was sending a smaller function of itself with the shuttle. It was hoped that it would be able to help them maintain contact and also serve as a backstop to the fact that they were all human and prone to errors.

Not that it could shut them down. But it could try to talk them down. And it could assume control of the shuttle if something catastrophic happened.

Lt. Dish appeared in the launch bay, flanked by Tim and Trac, who seemed to be carrying her gear for her. Trac didn't have gear—unless the skitterfin counted as gear—but Tim did or should, despite his remaining cybernetics.

The warmth from their brief moment of real contact faded at the sight of the lieutenant. Like she and Tim, Lt. Dish had donned Garradian interstellar flight gear—rated for in and out of atmosphere. But she didn't look like them in that gear. She looked…more.

Riina suppressed a sigh and turned back to checking their gear.

"I believe the alien entity deployed an electromagnetic pulse against the planet," Veirn said.

Riina paused and glanced at the others, but they didn't react. So Veirn was speaking just to her. She waited until they'd moved deeper into the shuttle and said, "So it disabled their electronics. Power, etc?"

"Correct. The blackout appears to be planet-wide. If I am reading the data correctly, this would not just shut down their electricity but ground all their vehicles."

That would restrict movement and affect communications. Dr. Walker had been left with a land flyer, but that would be down as well.

"Do you think we'll be affected by it when we pass under the entity?"

"This shuttle is protected from EM weapons, but it will make communicating with Dr. Walker and Harold…challenging."

"We know where they were supposed to be," Riina said. "We'll have to start there, I guess."

"We also have a known location he was communicating from, but it is a considerable distance from our rendezvous point."

Riina blew out a breath. "And they might have trouble traveling after the EM weapon was used. I guess we have to assume it was a weapon? A hostile act?"

"I am always," Veirn said, "reluctant to make assumptions. It is against my programming to assume. However, I am able to postulate that it appears to be a hostile act."

The AI was threading a very small needle there, but Riina couldn't argue with its logic.

"We need to try to avoid escalating things."

"I agree," Veirn said. "But much will depend on the reaction of the inhabitants."

"And what the alien entity is doing with its advantage."

Their sensors couldn't see through the alien miasma, which was troubling. What was happening down there?

Riina felt urgency rise. She turned and strode toward the bridge.

"We need to get going," she said.

11

If it hadn't been for the two moons, the darkness would have been eerily intense, though Miles' night vision was slowly returning after the brilliant flashes from what he presumed were weapons.

"What just happened?" Lira asked, her voice a whisper, as if the aliens might overhear them.

"I think it was an EM pulse," he whispered back. Okay, he was a bit freaked out, too. "Harold?"

Had the EM pulse taken the robot down with the rest of the electronics? It was starting to seep into his consciousness just how very hosed they were. If their comms were down, their flyers most likely were, too.

They'd brought emergency supplies in their flyer, but how hard would it be to access the interior with the electronics out?

And—bigger question—now that the aliens had put out the lights, what did they intend to do with their advantage?

"I am in the process of rebooting my systems," Harold said, its voice back to its most robotic yet.

"How bad were you hit?" Miles asked. He hadn't been sure the robot could answer him, and it wasn't over the comms.

Somehow, in the scramble for cover, it had landed next to him. Or had joined him? And where was Lira's father?

"I experienced some disruptions before I deployed counter measures."

Miles hadn't known there were counter measures for an EM pulse. He resisted the urge to find out more. They had larger problems to resolve.

Problem one. Depending on how badly their communications were damaged, he had no way to get in contact with the *Quendala.*

Problem two. They were a considerable distance from Lira's house, and their flyers were most likely out of commission.

Problem three. Their emergency supplies were inside the flyers and possibly inaccessible, though if Harold was able to recover it was possible it could break into their flyer.

Problem four. If the planet was experiencing an alien invasion, he only had an electronic—and probably disabled—ray gun to defend them with.

And what was that thing that had seemed to suck the Vorthari right out of the ground? It hadn't been a gentle extraction either.

That didn't seem like a hostile act. But the EM pulse? That did seem hostile. Unless it had to do with the Vorthari? Were they somehow affected by electronic signals?

He didn't know what the nanites had done to neutralize the Vorthari they'd encountered at the southern pole.

There was, he admitted rather ruefully, a lot he didn't know. And it wasn't all just because he was a geologist and far out of his scientific lane.

"What do we do now?" Lira's voice had a tremble to it.

She'd had to process a lot since her first contact with Miles and Harold. He'd gone in knowing the planet was inhabited by —to him—aliens, and he couldn't say he was loving everything that had happened.

Except for meeting her. He turned and their gazes met. Okay, worth it. But still stressful.

"So," Lira's father's voice came from the other side of Lira, "these aren't your people?"

There was, Miles noted, a hint of disbelief in his voice.

"Totally not my people," Miles said. "In any way, shape or form, not my people."

Slowly more shapes appeared out of the darkness. Miles risked his flashlight on its lowest beam. Thank heavens it was an old fashioned, non-electronic version that he carried as a matter-of-course.

With some unease, Miles realized that some of the shapes had deployed their weapons. The one Lira had called Drun was central to the weapons carrier group. He was going to make a wild guess that these weapons weren't electronic and still working. Oh good, jumpy, scared, and possibly trigger-happy inhabitants. His favorite thing.

"This is your people's peaceful arrival?" The scorn in the voice was unsettling.

At least he was looking at Harold. But he noticed people were starting to eye him with suspicion. Apparently yelling at them to take cover was now going to be considered a hostile act.

"These are not my people," Harold said. "That was not the ship we were expecting."

"We?" Drun said, his gaze shifting toward Miles. "You are with him, aren't you?"

It would be challenging to do an autopsy on him in the current circumstances, so he nodded.

"But Harold is correct, these are not our people. No way our people would have fired on us." Had they fired on us? On the planet? It felt more like they'd sucked up the Vorthari. That didn't seem hostile.

None of the weapons wavered. It was possible they were

experiencing trust issues. He certainly felt a disconnect between what he'd expected and what they'd just experienced.

Another figure approached Drun.

"Our vehicles have been disabled."

Miles was pretty sure that was Pollin.

"The entity deployed an electro-magnetic pulse," Harold said. "Electronics may reboot. Or not."

There was an unhappy murmur from the group around them.

"Maybe don't be so blunt with the bad news delivery," Miles murmured to Harold. Louder he added, "Let's let Harold here take a look at our vehicles. He might be able to help."

Before Harold could dispute this, Miles gave him a very pointed look.

"You can examine them, can't you, Harold?"

There was a pause, then Harold said, "Very well."

Even with the robotic tone, Miles heard the lack of encouragement.

"You will wait here," Drun said. "Watch him." A pause and then in a hardened tone, "Watch them."

"Drun?" Lira's father sounded outraged.

Miles could have told him that the proper response might be an "*et tu, Brute.*" Or at least their version of it.

12

Tim activated the shuttle's cloaking as they cleared the *Quendala's* cloak. He'd talked to Rinna and Captain Kellen about the pros and cons of using the phased cloak to just pass through the entity, but neither of them was sure that the cloak would react well with that entity or within it.

It was a complete unknown so far. They'd even been reluctant to insert probes for fear of giving their presence away.

As their shuttle passed by it, they scaned it as much as they dared, but their main mission, their main goal, and still their primary mission, was to make contact with Dr. Walker and Harold and extract them from the planet's surface.

Their secondary mission was to assess the Vorthari problem. It had been a long shot when they set out and now it seemed to be an even longer one.

They would, Tim thought, as he set a course that would keep them clear of the entity, be fortunate if they could make contact with Dr. Walker.

Despite the problems they faced, Tim felt at peace. Riina sat in the copilot's seat next to him. It was both familiar and comforting—as long as he didn't look at his human components.

He had enough cybernetics to allow him to connect with the shuttle in a manner that enhanced his human responses, assisted by Veirn. His connection was still somewhat slower than previously, but again, could be ignored. What was it, this bit of Veirn, he wondered. What should he call it?

Trac sat at navigation and was fully connected to the shuttle systems. Lt. Dish sat behind Riina, not connected to anything. Her controls weren't live, just in case she forgot and touched something.

Tim was aware that Trac was feeding data to her screen, however. Perhaps he didn't want her to feel left out. Did humans need data as much as he and his crewmates did? He had not been human long enough to know if he'd brought this need with him to his body, or if it was also a human quality.

"Will we try to make radio contact with Dr. Walker?" Lt. Dish finally asked, breaking what had been a long silence.

Riina glanced back at her. "As near as we can tell, the planet was hit with an electro-magnetic pulse. This would have taken down all comms."

"Oh, right."

Another silence formed. Tim didn't remember being bothered by silence before, but could he call what he'd experienced "silence," when his flow of data had never been interrupted?

"So, what's the plan?" Again it was Lt Dish who spoke.

"We will proceed to our original rendezvous point," Tim said. "It is possible Dr. Walker will still be there, since the pulse would have also disabled his flyer."

"If he has changed location, perhaps attempted to hike out," Rinna spoke this time, to Tim's satisfaction, "then his next logical action would be to return to the habitation where he and Harold were staying."

"Hike out?" Lt. Dish sounded puzzled.

"We, of necessity, had them chose a remote location, so as to avoid locals," Riina explained.

Tim liked the sound of her voice, and it was a bonus that she sounded less constrained than she'd been since his reintegration.

"But he made contact," Lt. Dish said.

"With two locals, yes, but hopefully that is all his interaction has been," Riina said. "First contact is tricky and dangerous. We can, fortunately, speak the language, so that shouldn't be a problem, but we'd like to avoid a wider interaction until we have more data on the Vorthari problem."

"It seems like that would build some goodwill with the locals," Lt. Dish said. "It sounds like they headed off a bad situation."

"It's not that simple," Riina said. "From their perspective, it might look like Dr. Walker blew something up. We do have the video of his interactions, but will they believe it? A lot depends on their sophistication and their level of video abilities."

"They could think we faked it," Lt. Dish said, her tone thoughtful. "I hadn't thought of that. But we do have deep fakes back on Earth."

The shuttle alerted Tim to his next course correction. They were traveling around the furthest edge of the entity now. He watched both scanning and the actual view from the shuttle's forward windows.

The entity looked even more unsettling than it had appeared from what was the top or overhead.

No light penetrated into it or from out of it, but he sensed shape and form. It was particularly eerie hanging as it did over the dark planet, lit only by the furtive light of its two moons.

"We do have life signs from the planet."

Riina sounded relieved. Whatever it was the entity had done, it hadn't killed the inhabitants of Arroxan Prime.

Yet.

And if they were here to kill everyone? They might be able

to get to Dr. Walker, but how did they stand by and watch a world's worth of people die?

————

"Preparing to leave orbit," Tim said.

Riina checked the systems, feeling an unfamiliar worry. They wouldn't just be leaving orbit. They'd be entering atmosphere and having their first look underneath the entity.

She felt the shuttle shift as Tim adjusted their trajectory. Then the slight resistance as they slid into upper atmosphere.

"I'm going to fly parallel at first, so we can take some readings."

Outside the ship, fire flared as the atmosphere resisted their entry.

It felt like it took too long for it to taper off.

"A heavy atmosphere?" she asked.

"It shouldn't be this heavy," Tim said.

And suddenly they were in the clear.

Or not.

Ahead, it was bright and light, but off to their left, the entity region was dark and foreboding—but also lit with bright flashes of light.

Riina triggered the main sensors and directed them toward the darkness.

It took time for the readings to begin to register, but when they did, she frowned.

"It's firing on the surface," Rinna said. "Those are surface impacts." She brought up some other readings. "Yes, impacts in addition to the seismic activity. Or are they? It almost appears as if something is being extracted from the surface."

Out of the corner of her eye, Riina noted Tim's frown.

"Is there a pattern? It's going to be difficult to fly in there," he said.

"Should we try?" she asked the question because she must. They had to get in there.

Now Tim looked surprised. "Of course."

Riina bit back a smile. His response didn't surprise her. Tim, like all his crewmates, didn't see roadblocks, just obstacles to get over, around, or through.

It was, she realized somewhat ruefully, one of the things she liked about him. Liked? Yes, *liked*, she told herself firmly. And tried not to look at the strong arms so sure and commanding on the controls.

Unfortunately, not looking at his arms somehow brought her gaze to his profile. Firm jaw. Stern gaze. And his lips…

She yanked her attention back to her screen.

"The impacts are increasing, but I think I see a pattern." She pulled up another data set. "I think they are focused on areas where the seismic activity is the strongest." She went through the data more slowly. "Yes, I think there is a pattern. If I'm right, there is a flight path. A possible flight path. It's still a risk."

"Why is it a risk?" Lt. Dish asked.

But it was Trac who answered her. "If a new area of seismic goes active while we're over it…"

"Oh."

Riina sensed she shifted in her seat.

"Shall I keep focused on the seismic then?"

Riina couldn't help her look of surprise in Tim's direction. He shrugged.

"All right."

"I will monitor the entities' firing patterns," Trac said. "They seem to be able to fire from multiple locations, but sensors aren't able to discern weapons arrays yet."

"Or any discernibly discrete ships," Riina muttered. It remained, to the sensors, a miasma with a widely dispersed energy signature.

As she studied the data, she initiated a database search for anything comparable. She not only had access to the Garradian data, both past and present, but also the *Najer's* databanks. At least what they'd shared.

Had they shared all they knew? There was no real way to know, but she wanted to believe they had. And not just because she considered Tim a…friend.

Their comm crackled and then she heard Nevv's voice.

"An update, please, Riina," he said.

"We're still collecting data before we penetrate under the entity," she said. "We're getting some interesting—and frankly confusing—data points. I'll shoot you what we've got in case we lose comms."

"Then you are going underneath it?" Nevv sounded worried.

"It's the only way to locate Dr. Walker," she pointed out, even though she knew Nevv already knew this. She glanced at Tim. "We're going in as soon as we have a solid flight path."

"I'm pulling up your transmit now," Nevv said. There was a long pause and then, "That doesn't look promising, Riina."

"Tim can handle it," she said. There was a touch of bravado in the words, but she also felt the truth of them. Tim could handle it and a lot more.

———

Tim did a mental countdown. He wasn't sure why. He activated thrusters and adjusted course. In atmosphere, the course adjustment happened faster.

The shuttle began to angle toward the darkness with its flaring lights.

He had a mental map, in addition to the screen tracking their course. The mental map had the impact pattern overlaying the map of the terrain they'd taken from the data Dr. Walker had sent.

He wondered how much it had changed since the arrival of the entity. Trac was also sending him data he'd parsed, separate from what the ship was delivering. It did look as if the entity was extracting something, even as it also fired down on the planet. Or after firing? That was also possible.

The shuttle's lights came on as they left natural light behind. He'd considered going in dark, but it seemed like a bad idea. Of course, so did going in lit.

"There's new seismic beginning to show up. I've sent the heading to your screen," Lt. Dish said.

Tim watched a weapon's track suddenly head toward the new location. Was the entity attacking the seismic locations?

Tim considered what they'd learned from Dr. Walker's findings. There had been increased seismic at that location, too. Was there a correlation?

"Why is the thing firing on the seismic locations?" Lt. Dish asked. "The impacts don't seem to be reducing the activity. If anything it is increasing it."

"Could they be trying to destabilize the planet?" Riina said. "It's already a very challenging planet to inhabit."

"It wouldn't be hard to destabilize it," Veirn's fragment said.

Tim let his agreement with this statement pass through his thoughts which were mostly focused on avoiding flying into the path of the weapons' fire.

"Any new data on what kind of energy they are deploying?" Tim asked.

Data popped up, courtesy of Trac. He'd always been on point that way. Tim had a sense that Veirn's fragment might be annoyed by Trac's speed.

"That's some serious fire power," Lt. Dish commented.

Had Trac sent the data to her, too? Well, obviously he had,

but why? Tim still wasn't quite sure what her function was on the team. It seemed to be a moving target.

"It appears to be designed for deep planetary penetration," Trac said.

"Heads up," Lt. Dish said suddenly. "New seismic directly ahead."

Tim banked the shuttle. Felt it rock as the energy bean passed close to them. Too close? The hairs on the back of his neck were standing up, and the air seemed to crackle with expended power. He sensed Veirn's fragment enhancing his ability to respond. It was both odd and almost familiar, harkening back to his time as a cyborg.

"How far to Dr. Walker's last known location?" Lt. Dish asked.

"If we don't have to detour too much, we should be there in under an hour," Tim said.

"There's…"

Tim banked the shuttle sharply, not waiting for Lt. Dish to finish her new warning. This time he banked the other direction. The shuttle rocked more forcefully this time and a warning light popped up on the console.

"That one singed us," Riina said, her voice remarkably calm.

Tim checked. It was an apt description.

"How much damage?" Riina asked, her voice low.

"Just a glancing hit, a singe." He flashed her a quick smile. "We'll be fine."

If everything went well, they'd be fine, but one thing he had learned. Humans didn't like their "fine" to be qualified.

He'd connected himself to the seismic. They couldn't afford to wait for Lt. Dish to give warning.

"I think we're passing over a city," Riina said. "I'm showing life signs, lots of them. Will we have trouble picking up Dr. Walker's life sign, do you think?"

"Not if the location is as isolated as he claimed it would be," Tim said.

————

Riina held onto the sides of her seat, even though she was firmly strapped in. She was reminded of the thing called a video game that one of the Expedition members had shown her.

She'd played it well enough but had thought it not realistic.

Now, she would have been happy for less realism.

Swiftly changing angles as they hurtled forward.

Spasms of light in multiple colors both in the sky and falling from the sky.

Earth heaving upwards at each hit. Then the surge that came after the hit, as if something were being sucked upwards.

And they were dodging both that from above and that from below.

They got "singed" more than once. More warning lights appeared on the controls, but Tim's attention never wavered.

Riina knew he was probably receiving data both visually and through implants. If he weren't, they'd probably already have been a smoking hull on the ground.

"Why," Lt. Dish's voice sounded strained, "are they attacking this planet? It seems pretty harmless to me. A little crazy with all the seismic, but harmless. It's not like they are near enough to anyone to cause problems. And didn't you say they weren't space capable yet?"

The flood of questions breaking the silence was probably more about release of tension than a true desire for answers.

Plus, Riina didn't have answers to her questions. They had access to the same data.

"There is the Vorthari," Trac pointed out.

"But they are underground," Lt. Dish said.

"They are targeting areas of high seismic activity," Riina

reminded them, gritting it out as Tim made a series of twisting turns that left her feeling like she'd been tied in knots.

And, if Dr. Walker's data was correct, his interaction with the Vorthari had been in an area of high seismic.

"They might be after the Vorthari, and not the inhabitants of Arroxan Prime," she said. It wouldn't be much comfort to the people down below, lost in the dark and under attack.

But if the Vorthari were the target, based on what she saw? There were a lot of them.

"They would have avoided building on those areas," she said, as much to comfort herself as them. But the area in the pole where Dr. Walker had arranged their meetup was also registering seismic. Or follow-on explosions.

"We might be too late," she said.

Tim didn't look at her. He couldn't. But she saw his lips thin. He didn't like losing any more than she did.

13

It wasn't much of a relief when they came within scanning range of the rendezvous point.

There were no life signs detected and the actual meet point coordinates still showed heat from the attack.

He brought the shuttle in as low as he dared over the site and turned on video to add to their scan data. Wisps of smoke still drifted up into the frigid air. A blackened circle had been carved out of the surrounding ice cover surface. And there might be a hole at its center. It was hard to tell.

There were no visible bodies.

"What's that?" Riina asked, zooming a camera in on dark shapes off to one side of the impact crater.

Tim angled their path over the shapes so the cameras could get better views.

"Those are flyers. Ground vehicles perhaps," she said.

"I am unable to connect with Dr. Walker's flyer," Veirn's bit said over the comms. "All systems are completely offline."

"I should check them out," Trac said.

Tim wanted to object, but he'd have to gear up for the frigid temperatures and there was also a risk of atmospheric contamination left over from the attack.

He gave a sharp, reluctant nod and brought the shuttle down as close to the vehicles as he dared.

"What about...?" Tim wasn't sure what to call the skitterfin, so he pointed at it.

"Fred will stay here with you," Trac said.

Fred?

Trac lowered his arm until he touched Tim's shoulder and the skitterfin unfolded its wings and three tails, scampered down Trac's arm and wrapped itself around Tim's neck.

He didn't like it. It wasn't painful, but the skitterfin was quite warm. And a bit prickly.

"Can I go, too?" Lt. Dish asked.

"No," Trac said, activating the hatch and passing back into the rear of the shuttle.

The hatch hissed closed, leaving an awkward silence behind.

"He can act quickly," Tim said, finally. "Without waiting for us to don suitable gear."

"Oh." Lt. Dish paused. "Right. That makes sense."

"I'm still not picking up any life signs," Riina said, "though the extreme cold might be masking them if they are geared up and on foot."

It was a hopeful assessment, but right now all they had was hope.

The rear hatch registered as lowering, after a pause, he watched Trac approach the small array of flyers. None showed any sign of power, which made sense following the electromagnetic strike. But in the light from Trac's headlamp, he saw that two of the flyers' doors hung open.

"I believe Harold accessed these flyers for supplies," Trac said over the comms.

"Why Harold?" Riina asked.

"Only a robot could have broken into these vehicles," Trac answered.

He was now surveying the ground around the vehicles. If Harold had survived the attack, then hope could turn into a small certainty. There was no reason for the robot to acquire supplies unless there was a human with him.

"I believe multiple humans walked this direction," Trac said, pointing with his arm and his light.

It was in the general direction of the closest habitations. But it was an optimistic move. It was a long hike in the darkness.

"I'm going to follow the trail," Trac said. "Follow me from the air."

Tim didn't like that, but again, it was the best option. Had he still been a cyborg, it was what he'd have done.

"I don't like it," Riina said.

"No," Tim agreed. So far, there was nothing to like about this planet or their current situation. The skitterfin made a noise in his ear. Did that mean it agreed with him? He reached up and touched its nose. The skitterfin seemed to rub the tip of his finger.

At least it hadn't bit him.

————

Tim, Riina noted, kept the shuttle at its slowest hover speed, but they still had to circle back to Trac when they got too far ahead of him.

"How far could they have gotten from our rendezvous location?" she asked, not really expecting an answer.

There was too much they didn't know, about the planet's topography, about the timing of the attack, about who had been with Harold and Dr. Walker (the correct answer should have been nobody or just the side chick), how well their gear could protect them and whether it could shield them from life signs detection.

After being attacked, they would be attempting stealthy progress—or they should be. She'd have been keeping her head down.

The presence of the other flyers troubled her. Who and how many others had known about their impending arrival?

Was it happenstance or deliberate choice that the attack had commenced before they could get there? Had this alien entity known they were coming?

They'd made no attempt to contact them, so either they didn't care, didn't know or…planned to deal with them later.

She couldn't, she realized wryly, blame them if they didn't see the *Quendala* as a threat. It wasn't a ship of war, though it was well-supplied with weaponry. And it was cloaked, she reminded herself. Odds were that the entity couldn't detect it.

And the question after that? Was it well supplied with the *right* weaponry?

"There is no way to know this," Veirn—or Veirn's snippet said.

It took Rinna a minute to figure out which question it had answered. Inside her head, she'd already moved on.

"Yeah," she said, to let Veirn know she'd heard it. Then she resumed her own thoughts. They'd never encountered anything like the entity, so how did she know if anything they carried would work against it if it turned out to be hostile to them? Or that the cloak would work against it?

"I wish we knew if any population centers have been impacted," she said. She didn't see how the planet could get by without some losses, even if the entity was trying to avoid populations. And right now, there was no way to know if that was the case.

"I have found them," Trac said, suddenly.

Fred lifted its head, peering out the front window and his

wings shifted slightly. He made that soft sound again. Rinna glanced at him, but he was looking forward. Trac wasn't currently in sight. They were once more ahead of Trac and had to circle back to find the cyborg standing in a circle of what appeared to be armed humans. Humans all pointing their weapons at Trac.

Fred made a sound that seemed scornful to Riina.

It was brave of them to point weapons at Trac, she conceded. It was a good thing that he was, for a cyborg, pretty chill. He'd even lifted his arms in an attempt to appear non-threatening.

It was a vain attempt, of course. He wasn't the scariest of the cyborg models, but they didn't know that. And he didn't have to be. All he had to be was who he was.

No one had, as yet, fired on him. That didn't mean they wouldn't panic and start. It wasn't a huge worry. Nothing they were aiming at him would even make a dent.

"Dr. Walker?" Riina figured it was worth a try, though the EM pulse must have surely fried his comms. It wasn't a surprise when Harold answered.

"Dr. Walker is unable to communicate," it said.

"But he and you are okay?" Riina persisted.

"We are not dead," Harold said. "Dr. Walker has been secured with local restraints. He is worried about becoming an alien autopsy."

It wasn't clear if Harold shared that worry or not.

"Our planetary contacts, Lira and her father, are also under restraint. Most of these humans are not official representatives of the government, but there is one." And then Harold added, "I would assess them all as what Earthlings would call trigger happy. Approach with caution."

———

Riina wanted to go out alone to meet the group of humans. She thought she looked less threatening. If that were her criteria, then they should send Lt. Dish out, Tim thought.

Tim didn't, however, say this out loud. He may be new to being a human, but even he knew it would be a bad idea.

"They might like a hot guy," Lt. Dish said. "You never know."

Tim blinked. Who was the hot—oh. He glanced at Riina and she grinned and shrugged.

"She might have a point."

"I think I should go," Lt. Dish said.

"Why?" Rinna asked.

"No reason. I'd just like to make first contact. It would be cool."

This time the look Riina gave him was mixed with humor and wry. It was a good look on her. He wished…

He looked away. "We should call Trac back."

"What about Dr. Walker?" Lt. Dish sounded alarmed now.

"I will go negotiate with them," Tim said.

"I need to go, too, but Tim is right. We need Trac back on board."

Trac could fly the shuttle and protect Lt. Dish if things went south.

Tim sent the recall code to Trac. He probably should have taken time to assess the situation better. Trac turned, possibly in mid-sentence and walked back to the shuttle, humans scattering to clear his path.

No one shot at him. That was a positive.

He unstrapped and found it interesting that Fred transferred to Lt. Dish. She looked startled but also pleased. She reached up and ran a finger down from the top of his head to the tip of his nose. Did this make Fred purr?

He left the cockpit and went to don protective gear, aware

that Riina was close behind him. He thought Lt. Dish offered a mild protest. If she had, he ignored her.

Riina rushed to gear up, but he still finished before her. He picked up her headgear and held it out to her. They had both lowered their headgear over their faces before the ramp lowered again for Trac to enter. Tim checked the temperature of the air rushing in and was grateful he was protected.

Trac thumped up the ramp and joined them.

"What is the problem?" he asked.

"We need you to protect the shuttle," Tim said, "while we try to talk to the humans." He knew he shouldn't call them humans, or rather, that he was a human, too, so it might be weird, but it was a hard habit to break.

"Right." Trac waited by the hatch to the cockpit. He wouldn't open it until the ramp were up again. The bitter cold rushed in and seemed to fill every inch of the bay. It was interesting that none of the humans attempted to board or even close on the shuttle. He knew this because he had a view from the front of the shuttle playing on one of his implants. They were all still milling around and possibly arguing, based on the erratic movements of their arms.

"It would be better," he said to Riina, "if you stayed here." It was futile. He knew this, but he had to try.

"Better for whom?"

He blinked. "For me," he said, before he could stop himself.

Her eyes widened. "For you? How?"

"I worry," he admitted.

Her expression softened. "I worry, too. So, we'll both have to be careful."

"We are always careful," he pointed out. "And things still happened."

She grinned. "True. But we're still here." She hesitated, as if she wished to say more, but she didn't. She turned and headed toward the ramp. It took two strides for him to reach — and then pass her. If he couldn't stop her, then he could shield her.

———

Riina didn't know why she felt so encouraged by Tim's words as they tromped down the ramp and then began to crunch across the ice toward the small, agitated bunch of — humans. She grinned at Tim's designation. He hadn't quite embraced his own humanity.

The sky overhead was still dark and ominous, with flickers of light briefly appearing, then disappearing. There was an almost constant rumble underfoot, distant, but omnipresent.

Only the lights from their headgear cut decisively through the darkness. Her suit registered a serious level of cold, and she wondered how the small band was managing their long trek. Even a Garradian suit would begin to struggle over the length of time it would take them to reach human habitation once more. Did they have proper gear?

She wondered what they thought as their two points of light approached. When her light reached them, they'd formed into more of a wall of people, with one man — clearly their leader — at the center and facing them with his weapon lifted.

She held up her hands, hoping they could get close enough for the man to see that they were human, too.

Her suit could probably withstand a hit or two, but they'd still hurt. She hated getting shot.

"Don't come any closer."

The leader lifted his weapon warningly. Tim stopped and she did, as well, when they were side by side.

The man spoke in Arroxan Prime's main language, but her suit was able to translate it quickly, thanks to Dr. Walker sharing his updates with them.

"I would like to speak to Dr. Walker," Riina said. His condi-

tion would determine their next actions. If he'd been injured…
well, that wouldn't bode well for future interactions.

"He is fine."

"Then he can tell me that himself," Riina said, keeping her
voice mild, but firm.

The man turned and gestured. The crowd shifted and Dr.
Walker was shoved—not gently—into view.

"Are you well, Dr. Walker?" She spoke in Arroxan Prime. It
seemed wise to try to keep tensions from spiraling out of
control.

"They haven't cut me open yet," he said.

The group murmured and some shifted in place.

"Cut you open?" She tried to keep the surprise out of her
voice. She'd seen no sign that they were cannibals.

"Haven't you ever heard of an alien autopsy?" Dr. Walker
asked.

"I have," Tim said unexpectedly. He glanced at her. "One of
Dr. Walker's people showed me something called *The X-Files*."

"We have no plans to cut you open," the leader said angrily,
"though it would be no more than you deserve for deceiving
us."

"I didn't deceive you," Dr. Walker protested. "That wasn't
us. Those are us. Totally different."

"Dr. Walker is speaking the truth," Riina said. "We are as
unsettled by the arrival of the entity as you are. It is outside our
experience."

"I'm sure it will not surprise you to learn that we do not
believe you," the leader said.

"That's Drun," Dr. Walker said. "He's a Fed."

His tone said that explained everything and perhaps it did to
him. For Riina? Not so much.

"Drun Marik," Drun said huffily. "And I am not a Fed,
whatever that is."

"If you don't know what it is, how do you know you're not

one?" Dr. Walker's tone was reasonable, but there was definitely a hint of humor in it.

Drun spluttered for a few seconds, then said, "It does not matter. We came to the rendezvous in peace, and we were met with destruction. We do not know how widespread it is or if any of our people remain alive."

"We observed concentrations of life signs as we entered your atmosphere," Tim said. "We are not certain, of course, but it appears as if the entity is targeting what you call the Vorthari."

"We don't know what the Vorthari are, so we can hardly call it anything," Drun said and then seemed to realize his statement wasn't helpful. "But that is not relevant either."

"I think it's relevant," Dr. Walker said. "Lira and I had a very unfriendly interaction with the Vorthari and if that thing up there is after them, then that's a good thing."

Dr. Walker wasn't wrong, but he also wasn't entirely correct. Riina sighed. The people of Arroxan Prime could end up as collateral damage if it came to a fight between the Vorthari and the entity.

They needed to find a way to make contact with it. She had known this since their first sighting, but she hadn't wanted to risk their rescue of Dr. Walker. Now that he was relatively safe, it seemed like a good idea to try to make contact.

Of course, a lot of things had seemed like a good idea during past missions and turned out to be not so good, so she wasn't in a hurry.

"Your flyer is still working." A man pointed at it. "How is that possible if you're not working with what attacked us?"

"We weren't in your atmosphere when they deployed the EM pulse," Tim said.

There was another murmur.

"You are from away?" This was a woman's voice and fear threaded through it.

Riina felt the disconnect between the woman's tone and her showing up to meet and greet actual aliens. Had she not really believed it was going to happen?

"Yes," Riina confirmed the obvious. "We are from away, but not the same away as the entity. We've never encountered anything like it before." Or anything like the Vorthari, for that matter.

Tim glanced at her, as if he felt he should speak to her first, but then he turned back to Drun Marik.

"It is a long walk to the nearest habitation. We will give you a lift. And you will release the restraints on Dr. Walker."

Riina glanced around, wondering if they'd tried to restrain Harold, too. But the robot suddenly eased between the small group.

"It is a good plan," Harold said.

Riina saw that he had strapped supplies onto his back. She wanted to ask or say something about the fact that they appeared to trust the alien robot, but not the alien man. But it was also not truly relevant.

It was clear that they didn't want to accept the lift. And also clear that they knew they'd have to.

"We will stand surety for Dr. Walker's behavior," Riina said. "And you, Drun Marik, may examine the interior before your people board, if that would help. If it simply what we call a shuttle—a craft designed to shuttle people from one place to another."

Drun stared at her for a long moment, then looked up. "You have a ship up there somewhere."

It wasn't a question, but Riina nodded.

"We have a ship up there," she agreed.

Now the murmur that ran through the small group sounded different, as if they all wished they could see it. At least, that is what she sensed.

Who were these people? How had they ended up at Dr. Walker's rendezvous point?

"Come," Tim said, gesturing to Drun.

But as the man moved forward, so did the little group.

"We want to see, as well," a woman said.

They rounded the rear of the shuttle in an odd clump, with Harold and Dr. Walker hanging back a little. Well, they'd both seen a shuttle before.

The group made sounds, but nothing that could be interpreted meaningfully.

"You can board, if you'd like," Riina said. "Take a seat on either side and we'll show you how to strap in."

"Strap in?" A different woman sounded alarmed.

"There is much…turbulence in the atmosphere," Tim said. "It is better not to fly around the shuttle bay. You could be injured"

The rear hatch was closing, increasing the muted alarm of the people. It was a relief that this reduced the amount of chill air flowing in. Riina felt the heat come on and let her faceplate go back.

With some caution, the group began to follow suit, taking tentative breaths.

The door to the cockpit slid back, revealing Lt. Dish in the opening. With some amusement, Riina noted the male spines straightening at the sight of her.

"Can I help?"

"Please," Riina said. She moved toward the end of the left row and was helping two people get strapped in when it happened.

A seismic disturbance rocked the shuttle. She staggered and felt herself gripped by Tim, her face pressed into his chest.

"Lifting off," Trac said tersely over the comm. "Hang on if you aren't strapped in."

Riina couldn't see who was and who wasn't secured. Tim's

arms tightened around her as the shuttle lifted off and accelerated forward.

How did he manage to brace himself? she wondered. She lifted her chin and caught him looking down at her, a look in his eyes that made her heart speed up.

"Riina." His voice was hoarse.

"Incoming," Trac called, over the comm and through the still open hatch.

The shuttle banked sharply. And this time it tumbled them —and everyone not secured—to the floor.

14

Tim twisted his body, so that Rinna fell on him and not on the metal flooring or on any of the others tumbling around them.

The lights flickered and he registered another side swipe singe them by whatever it was the entity was firing on the planet. The shuttle rocked, causing more of their passengers to emit cries of distress.

One arm around Riina, he grabbed the arm of someone sliding by him and stopped their movement.

He couldn't tell if Lt. Dish was okay, but when the lighting steadied, he saw her sitting on the lap of a man who did not look sorry to find her there.

Dr. Walker had a grip on the one he called Lira. Tim tipped his head to the side. The grip was what he'd call one of intent. And the look in their eyes also indicated intent.

He looked back at Riina, wondering if his gaze betrayed intent? He felt it. But did she feel the same intent for him? He met her gaze and his brain stalled. He hated to assume too much, but it rather looked like…intent.

The shuttle rocked from side to side again.

"We need to get people secured before someone gets seriously hurt," Riina said.

He told himself he heard regret in her tone and saw it filter into her gaze when he released her. He shifted her to the side, got up, and helped her up. They both turned to the task of helping their passengers get into seats and strapped down. Tim noted that Harold, who hadn't been tumbled in any direction, was also lifting people into seats and securing straps with detached efficiency.

Having been a robot himself, he wondered what Harold thought about all of this. But this was not the time to get a report from it.

Rinna directed Lt. Dish to get the first aid kit and then he suggested—also with intent—that both females return to the cockpit and strap in. He would finish up here.

Drun rose up in his face. If he'd been strapped in, he'd figured out how to get loose. Now he rocked with the shuttle's movement, grasping an overhead handle.

"I wish to monitor our progress," he stated with belligerence.

Tim nodded and pointed him toward the cockpit, then knelt in front of a woman who'd cut her head. He extracted materials to help. The woman next to her assisted him.

Their curious gazes made him uncomfortable, and he finally said, "What were you doing out here?"

They both looked surprised. "We came to meet aliens."

"Really?" He twisted to look at Dr. Walker. He'd understood from the briefing that no one knew they were coming except Dr. Walker, Lira and her father.

"It wasn't my fault," Dr. Walker said. "They picked up our transmissions and well, you heard her. They wanted to meet aliens."

Tim rose and looked around. One of the passengers had taken the first aid kit from him while he was working and passed it along the line, so that each injured person was able to tend their wounds.

Damage appeared to be fairly light. This was a relief. It could have been much worse. But Trac had tried to mitigate evasive action effects as much as possible. He was a better pilot than he would admit to. Of course, he very much disliked being at the helm. Tim did not know why. He liked piloting.

But since Trac didn't like piloting, he should relieve him.

Before he could act on that thought, he noticed that Lira had released her face plate and there was a bird head next to hers. He blinked, almost asked, then wasn't sure he wanted to know if she had two heads.

He made his way to the cockpit, stopping in the doorway and looking around. Riina, or possibly Lt. Dish, had directed Drun to a seat at the small science station. She was back at navigation and Rinna was in her co-pilot seat. Fred was back in his place around Trac's neck. Tim noticed that Drun was staring at the skitterfin with wide eyes.

"I can relieve you," Tim said. He stepped forward and the hatch slid closed. If this bothered their passengers, he didn't have to see it. He was already tired of them.

He'd been on missions gone wrong, more times than he cared to count up, but this one felt like it was just at the beginning of going wrong. His now human gut was twitching a wild and insistent warning of more trouble incoming.

Trac rose without complaint, surrendering the pilot seat to him. He continued to control the shuttle through his cybernetics until Tim was settled and able to take over, then transferred control—just in time for another round of extreme dodging.

He hadn't used to care about days or nights, but now he knew what the humans meant when they complained about how long the day had been.

It had been long and looked to only be getting longer. But…

he almost smiled. He'd held Riina in his arms for several whole seconds. And she'd looked like she didn't mind.

————

Out of the corner of her eyes, Riina noted Drun shifting in his seat. Well, he'd wanted this view. She could have told him that seeing what was incoming wasn't much fun, particularly when one lacked the power to control the dodges. Just when she'd start to relax, the firing from above began again.

"Were you injured?" she asked. That was also a possibility.

"Only a few bruises," he said, somewhat dismissively. His gaze flickered sideways to Trac and Fred. She wondered which bothered the man more. The cyborg or the skitterfin? He shifted again.

A few bruises, in the right section of his anatomy, could be as bad as a broken bone. It was only because of Tim's quick action, she wasn't sitting on some bruises. He'd cushioned her very…nicely.

She felt warmth suffuse her again. At the memory of being held. Of the way he'd looked at her. At the very human, very male way he'd looked at her.

She felt a sudden impatience for the mission to end, for them to be alone, for…talking. For clearing the air. She tended to forget how very inhuman it must have been for him to live for so long as a cyborg robot. How could he know the longings of her heart? How could he recognize them enough to act on them?

She hadn't wanted to take advantage of his, well, innocence, but that look he'd given her? That had been far from innocent.

Even as the shuttle was expertly steered into a wrenching dodge, she felt her lips edge up in a tiny smile.

A girl had to get her good moments where she could find them—especially one who'd spent a very long time frozen in stasis. She'd returned to life. She should be able to return to LIFE.

She looked at Tim and then stiffened. His muscles were bunching, as if he were struggling to control the shuttle.

"Trac," Tim gritted out.

"On it," Trac said.

Warning lights flared on every panel that Riina could see. The ones she couldn't see? She heard.

The cacophony was unpleasant and made it impossible to ask what was happening. She thought Drun might have tried. She saw his mouth moving.

The weird part? The shuttle wasn't lurching anymore. Their flight had smoothed out. And they were proceeding in a manner both level and...

She studied the controls.

She'd had some training as a pilot, but the readings exceeded her training. She'd almost have said they weren't proceeding at all. But that wasn't possible. No transport, not even a lowly shuttle could go from traveling at speed to stopped without the occupants feeling the transition.

The only useful thing she could think to do was to shut off the various warning sounds. One by one, they quieted until there was no sound left, just frantically blinking warning lights.

"What is happening?" Drun demanded, though his voice sounded less authoritative than it had.

"That is a good question," Lt. Dish said. There was a distinct quaver to her voice.

"We do not know," Trac said. His tone was of one stating the profoundly obvious.

Tim didn't speak, but Riina noted the slow lessening of tension in his shoulders. There was no lessening in the lines of his face.

He glanced at her. He didn't have to say it. She saw it in his eyes.

They were in trouble.

———

"Something is happening," Veirn said.

It had been so long since something had changed, that Nevv Kellen had allowed himself to be distracted. One could only study the same data sets for so long and not risk drifting off.

He glanced at the mission clock, noting how long they'd been out of touch with the shuttle.

"What?" Kellen asked.

"I believe the entity is contracting. It is very slight, but it is reading as smaller," Veirn said.

If they were preparing to leave…

"Should we try to make contact with them? With it?"

Veirn was silent for longer than was typical for the AI. Kellen knew it was running the various possible scenarios, so it could provide Kellen with a statistical analysis of which might be the best option.

But this time it was taking longer than usual. Much longer. As the seconds ticked by, Kellen began to see the shrinking of the entity on his screens as well.

If it was preparing to leave, they'd need to attempt contact soon.

While he waited, he tried to contact their team. If the entity's presence was lessening…

Nothing. Not even a slight ping.

Veirn actually sighed.

"There are too many unknown factors for me to give you a recommendation for or against attempting contact. You will have to go with," there was a pause like a human might make, "your gut."

Veirn hadn't liked saying that. Kellen would have grinned if the situation weren't so serious.

Kellen paused to try to read his gut. It felt as conflicted as Veirn.

"I'm going to try," he finally said. "We've tried sitting here and watching. We need to do something."

"I am attempting to open a channel with the entity," Veirn said.

The AI didn't mess around when a decision had been made.

"This is Captain Nevv Kellen of the Garradian ship the *Quendala*," he said, when he got the go ahead from Veirn. Kellen spoke, even while he noted that Veirn wasn't sure the connection had been made.

He was, quite literally, broadcasting into the cosmos.

––––––

The view outside the shuttle slowly dissolved into flickering lights. Tim had shut down the shuttle's engines, when he realized that they were having no impact and might be overheating.

Without the rumble of the engines, the cockpit felt wrong. The questions from the others were distant, almost muddy sounding. There was no sensation of movement, but never the less, he was certain they were moving.

Or changing locations.

Navigation was completely offline. So were sensors. Power and life support were both stable.

The lights outside began to settle into a flickering pattern and then even the lights slowly began to fade, leaving a dense darkness behind.

It reminded him of the darkness that had seemed to enclose the entity. Were they inside it? But how and why? And if not that, then what?

These kinds of questions were ones he usually left to his captain, or others higher up in the chain of command. His skill set consisted mostly of breaking things, shooting things, and flying things.

He became aware of an easing in the darkness, a different kind of light beginning to grow. It had a dark center, surrounded by shades of green and yellow.

No, it was two lights. It stopped closing on them and then a shutter came down over the lights and lifted again.

"I think," Riina said, her voice shaky, "those are…eyes."

He hoped she was wrong, but he feared she wasn't. In his experience, Riina was mostly correct in her deductions.

"I believe you are correct." Veirn's voice was a quiet contrast with the pounding of Tim's heart. He'd almost forgotten the AI fragment was on board, it had been quiet for so long.

"Eyes!" Drun's voice rose in pitch as if each letter were a single sound.

Fred made a sound that Tim felt could be interpreted as unhappy. He'd have made one, too, if his throat hadn't dried so completely.

The eyes did appear to be very large.

The eyes tilted, or the head that housed the eyes tilted to one side. If it was a head, it was a large one. Tim thought he saw a darker shadow below the eyes that could have been nostrils.

Then a gap appeared below the nostrils, and sound emerged.

Amazingly, the ship's translation program converted the words. Or it thought it had. How could they know?

"What is it?"

The original eyes eased back, and two more eyes came into view. It was still so dark that Tim couldn't see much detail beyond the eyes, possible nose, and mouth.

"It is a ship."

"But where from? I've never seen anything like it."

This voice was different. So, Tim's eyes didn't deceive him. There were two aliens regarding them. Them? Or the shuttle?

Tim wondered, a little vaguely, how the group in the rear of the shuttle would process these aliens? He kind of hoped he never found out. Hopefully they could resolve this without that happening.

"A ship would be carrying something."

"Yes."

Riina reached forward, her hand hesitating over the broadcast control, then she flipped the switch.

"Hello."

Hopefully the ship would translate this acceptably. If it didn't, things could go south very quickly.

Both sets of eyes blinked.

"Did it speak?"

"I believe it did."

The eyes moved closer to them and appeared to be studying them, if the up and down movement of the eyes were a correct indication.

"We are inside the object you are looking at," Riina said. "We are life forms."

One of the eyes came closer, until it was almost pressed up against their forward view screen. It blinked several times before it retreated.

"I believe there is something in here."

"The ship has passengers. Interesting."

"What if they get out?" The other voice was curious, not terribly concerned.

"We could get out, but we aren't certain we could survive." She said to Tim, "I also transmitted our requirements for life."

A large digit appeared out of the darkness and poked the shuttle. It rocked a little, not badly.

"You should not have gotten into our…"

The ship struggled with a translation, Tim noted.

"We did not mean to," Riina said. "We were on a mission to rescue some of our kind when we were intercepted by…you."

She glanced at Tim, and half shrugged.

"We will have to consult…"

Again, the translation failed.

"I'm guessing it, or they, are talking about their chain of command," Tim offered. He hoped he was correct. No question they were in a tight spot. And a weird spot.

Both sets of eyes faded back into the darkness.

"What was that?" Drun's voice made a demand, but it was, Tim decided more bravado than anything. "It, or they, were large."

The man must realize they were as confused as he was.

"Yes, they were," Tim agreed. He'd encountered larger aliens in his years aboard the *Najer*, but never anything like this. He had, he realized, picked the wrong time to become human again.

"What was it?" Drun asked again, though with a distinct quaver in his voice this time.

"There is no match in our database for the entity or entities," the Veirn fragment said. "But I am creating a file."

Somehow Tim didn't find this that comforting. For the file to be added to any larger database, they'd need to survive.

———

The entity had shrunk to what his systems said was its original configuration when they'd first spotted it.

They should have been able to make contact with their people now. It was no longer over the area identified as the rendezvous coordinates.

But still no contact.

The contact screen flickered several times, then steadied into…he wasn't sure what.

Something white filled the image with just a black circle in the center. There was sound, but nothing he recognized.

"I am attempting to translate," Veirn said. "It is a challenging language."

The AI had been designed to translate unknown languages, but even it needed time and content to do it.

The words switched as they came again.

"It is broadcasting in one of the languages of Arroxan Prime," Veirn said.

"Unknown vessel, it is advised not to approach the planet until it has stabilized from…"

There was something that Veirn obviously couldn't translate, even using the Arroxan Prime data.

"We have people down there," Kellen said, hoping they could retranslate what Veirn was sending. "We have been unable to make contact with them…"

But then the entity contracted to a small light and jumped away.

They were gone.

And there was no sign or sound of the shuttle and their people.

15

Rinna had many questions she wanted to give voice to, even though she was aware that none of those in the cockpit would have answers to those questions. She just wanted to ask them, to get them out, to stop them clogging her throat.

She was certain with the questions out of the way, the tightness in her chest would ease.

Well, not certain, just hopeful.

She and Tim had encountered some strange things in their travels together, but this might qualify as the strangest. She considered that, because it was a question she could answer herself.

The dragonfly alien they'd clashed with while on the mission with General Halliwell had definitely held the top spot and would retain that spot for its sheer lethality, for now.

She really hoped these wouldn't move up to that top spot. They hadn't seemed that hostile, just curious, so she had some hope.

But if the situation changed, at the moment it didn't seem like they had a lot of options to respond. She checked. Communications were offline. And as far as she could tell, without actually trying, so were weapons.

Not that she thought firing at this would be a good option just yet. But it would have been nice to have the option.

"What are they?" Drun persisted, though his tone moderated to almost reasonable. Perhaps he'd finally realized that hostility wasn't his best choice at the moment. That they were all in this—whatever this was—together. It did seem pointless to keep asking, when they'd all made it clear they didn't know, but humans—she included herself in that designation—were often unreasonable.

Riina felt a subtle shift under foot. She looked to Tim, trying not to let her alarm show. It felt a bit seismic, though much smaller.

"Something's coming," Tim said.

Did he realize he'd put his hand over hers? She wasn't sure, but she was grateful for the warm, very human touch of his hand over hers.

These eyes were much bigger than the last two. Much bigger. As it came closer, their view was reduced to just one, large eye.

Like the previous encounters, there was blinking and looking. And finally a question.

"Who are you?"

Riina paused, trying to order her thoughts. If there were gaps in their translation program, she needed to be very careful what she said. She would have been anyway, but this felt like more.

"We call ourselves humans," she said. She hesitated, but then didn't add more. Until they knew more, it didn't seem wise to identify where they came from. The legends about the lost Garradians had permeated farther than she'd expected.

"Humans." The pronunciation was a bit off. "How did you get into our…"

Again the translation failed.

"We are not sure," Riina said. She assumed, from the context, that they flown into the path of some kind of a collector. "As I said, we were on a mission to rescue several of our kind."

There were more of the blinks. It was unnerving to have the eye staring so intently into the ship. It was close enough she could see the variations in color and the pupil was sharply defined this close.

"Are there more of your kind?" It finally asked.

"There are many more on the planet," Drun said. "We live there."

"The planet." The voice sounded thoughtful. "Oh, you are the…"

Again a translation failure.

Did that mean the entity or whatever it was recognized that the planet did have inhabitants?

"You are not supposed to be here," it said.

"We didn't plan it," Riina said, a bit dryly, then wondered if it could hear tone. "If you could release us so we can go back to the planet…"

"That is no longer possible," it said. "We will soon arrive at…"

Rina had a feeling that this translation glitch was a serious one. Arrive where?

———

Tim cleared his throat and then spoke without looking at Riina. This was a breach of their protocol, but he'd had the sudden thought from watching the pattern of attack.

"Are you targeting the Vorthari? The entities that live under the surface of the planet?"

The eye blinked.

"Target? We don't know what this means. We clean out the infestation."

"That is what we came to do, too," Tim said. "At least, one of our kind cleaned out a nest of them prior to our arrival."

There was a distinct rumble, though whether it was a good sign, he didn't know.

"We wondered," it finally said. "But there are many more and they are waking and planning to leave."

"That was our assessment as well," Riina said, giving Tim and approving look. "Do they threaten the surface inhabitants? We understood that the Skaridrex contained them?"

"The Skaridrex have lost control. An interdiction was required."

"Is the interdiction dangerous to the surface inhabitants?" Riina asked the question again.

"The Vorthari are more dangerous. They would scavenge the surface life before moving on."

"But you can save them? The people on the planet?" This was from Lt. Dish.

Tim had almost forgotten she was there.

"Save them?" The voice sounded surprised. Or that could be the translation program projecting emotion. "They will save themselves. It will be easier now."

Drun gave a cry and tried to lunge out of his seat. The straps held him down and tightened in response to his lunge.

"No! Those are my people!"

"Could we perhaps consult on a way to rid the world of the Vorthari that allows the surface dwellers to survive?" Riina said hastily. "We were successful with the one nest of them."

"You do not understand," it said, "we have…" translation frizzed and then the eye retreated.

"I hope he doesn't take too long," Lt. Dish said. "It sounds like we don't have much time until something happens that I have a feeling we won't like."

"No," Riina agreed. "In the meantime, I'm going to try scanning and see if we can figure out just what this is. And where we are."

Tim opened his mouth to object. As far as he could tell, scanning was down.

"Could you get scanning back up, Trac?" Riina asked.

"My systems scanning is intact," Trac said. "I will share my data. It is, so far, puzzling and inconclusive. Perhaps I could refine it if I could egress the shuttle."

Tim jerked around to look at his friend. "Only if I go with you."

"We do not know if your gear can withstand the atmosphere outside the shuttle," Trac pointed out. "It could be toxic to both humans and their gear."

He was correct.

"How can you get out without letting that atmosphere in?" Lt. Dish asked.

He shifted his gaze to her, but it was Riina who answered.

"We have a one-person airlock."

"Those things were in the atmosphere," Drun said, still managing to sound annoyed.

"They are not human," Tim said, trying not to sound annoyed. Had they actually been in what contained them? Or had they projected their images? Knowing the answer might not change anything, he concluded. But he did wonder if they'd encounter any of them if they left the shuttle. That was a legitimate concern.

Trac had unstrapped and rose, though he could not attain his full height inside the cockpit. It was more like he unfolded as much of himself as space allowed.

"I will test the outer atmosphere. If it is non-corrosive to your gear, then you can join me," he said.

As if on some unspoken signal, Fred jumped back onto Lt. Dish's shoulder. Drun flinched back.

"I am uneasy with this course of action," Veirn's fragment said.

"We are all uneasy with it," Riina said. "But we need to do something."

"I suppose," Veirn said. It did not sound convinced.

Tim rose and followed Trac through the hatch to the bay of the shuttle. The airlock was just off the cockpit. The humans—with the exception of Dr. Walker—looked up in alarm at the sudden appearance of the cyborg. Tim wasn't sure why. They'd seen Trac outside. It had been in the dark, he conceded, and during a tense encounter. The sight of Tim right behind didn't seem to alleviate much of that alarm. If he'd had time, Tim might have been a little offended by that.

He caught a reflection of himself, with his cyborg eye. Oh. He tended to forget he still had cyborg enhancements that might be unsettling. Did that mean he was getting better at being human? Or just clueless?

He didn't have an answer for that question, so he wasn't sorry when Dr. Walker asked one.

"What's happening?"

Trac ignored him, his attention on preparing the airlock so he could enter it.

Tim opened his mouth. He closed his mouth. He blinked. Then he said, "Drun will explain."

He heard a muffled snort from behind him and grinned. He glanced back.

Riina had followed them into the bay and was trying not to grin.

Tim noticed that Drun hadn't followed them into the bay, as Trac opened the airlock and stepped inside. The hatch snapped shut and he heard the hiss of air being sucked out.

He was aware that Dr. Walker had unstrapped and walked over to peer into the cockpit.

"Whoa," he said. "I did not sign up for that."

For a few seconds, Tim feared he'd started a rebellion from their passengers. Indeed, they did shift their feet and murmur. But none of them unstrapped. He heard a bird squawk and looked around. It was a relief to realize that Dr. Walker's side chick didn't have two heads—one an avian head. He did wonder why they'd brought a bird to meet aliens.

It was possible they didn't know how to unstrap themselves, but Tim suspected there was an element of not wanting to know what was happening. He did not blame them for this. Knowing wasn't that great.

Tim heard the outer hatch opening, a sound confirmed by the controls. He stepped up and closed it, then began the process of equalizing it with their side.

"What's it like out there, Trac," he asked, when Trac didn't speak.

Instead of words, he received a file to his implants. He opened and studied the results. There was no question the outer atmosphere was hostile to humans, but it lacked the corrosive power to eat through his gear.

He dropped his faceplate and opened the now-ready airlock.

"Tim." Riina's voice was tense.

He looked at her, wished he knew how to use language that would reassure her. He wasn't human enough yet for that.

Perhaps she realized it because her lips trembled in a sort of smile.

"Be careful. Come back safely."

For her? He would try. He nodded and stepped into the narrow tube.

It was a good thing he wasn't claustrophobic. The hatch slid closed, brushing against his back. The air began to hiss out.

———

Rinna waited until she heard Tim declare himself clear, then turned back to the cockpit. She took the pilot's seat this time and worked on the video feed. After a period of reluctance, it flickered fitfully, then steadied, giving her a view of Tim and Trac standing a few feet from the shuttle's nose.

They didn't appear to be doing anything, but then she noted data arriving to her system from Trac.

She dragged her attention off the view of Tim and tried to focus on it. After a minute, she realized she didn't understand the readings. And she wasn't sure the ship's systems—including Veirn—knew how to read it either.

"Veirn?" she murmured. She kept her voice low to keep from further agitating Drun.

Veirn helped by picking out familiar elements and other readings, but there were a lot of unidentified stuff in there, too.

She could have used the bigger databanks on the *Quendala* right now, though she wasn't sure they would be a huge help if none of this matched with what they already knew.

Everything about this mission screamed not just first contact, but *first contact*. This entity or entities were new. Much of their elements were new.

She felt her breath huff out a bit at the thought of encountering something truly new. Though she hadn't herself experienced this, she'd been on site as new and interesting data had reached them from their research teams. It had caused enormous excitement. It was what fueled much of what they'd done. Had any of them been in a situation like this back then?

The Garradians had been about and been for research until…she sighed. Had they lost their courage and their curiosity during their long sleep?

She couldn't answer yet for her courage, but she could put her curiosity to work again. She could remember having it back in the day.

She bent her head to the data, her attention on the unfamiliar now. It was hard to concentrate with a clock ticking in her head—a clock she hadn't turned on but was still there.

What was going to happen soon? And why did she have a feeling that the entities were worried about it. Which meant she needed to worry, too.

16

"I believe," Trac said, "that this is some kind of containment bay. I detect limits in all directions."

Tim turned his head lamp on and made a slow three-sixty turn, but he saw nothing but the murky blackness.

"Are we alone in here?" He felt a stab of worry for the other humans on Arroxan Prime. He sensed the aliens considered anyone on the surface collateral damage. They'd made it clear they would have to save themselves from whatever it was they were doing on the surface.

"I am not sensing other life forms," Trac said.

"If we move out of sight of the shuttle, can we find our way back?" Tim asked. If they were just going to stand here, they might as well go back inside.

There was a pause. "I believe I can find the shuttle again," Trac said.

It was not as certain as Tim would have liked, but he realized that neither of them knew what would happen out here in this strange unknown with time possibly running out for them.

"We should use a lifeline," Trac said.

It was good advice. Tim pulled the attachment free of his suit and extended it to Trac, who hooked it to himself and then drew it through the hook to attach it to the shuttle. If, for some reason, the containment area lost gravity, it would keep Tim from floating away and should give them a way back to the shuttle

He frowned. There was gravity. That felt…odd, but then what wasn't odd about this situation?

"I am detecting a wall or field directly ahead. I propose we try that direction first," Trac said. "Then we can follow it around."

"Sounds like a plan," Tim said.

They walked a few feet before Tim asked, "Do you have comms with the shuttle?"

He did not. And Tim did not like it.

"For now," Trac said.

With that, Tim would have to be content.

They walked a few yards and then Trac held up a hand, stopping Tim.

"It is an energy field, not a physical wall," Trac said.

"Designed to shock or kill?" Tim asked.

"To kill," Trac said.

So, they wouldn't be going out that way, if by some chance they could get their engines to fire up.

Trac turned to the left and began to follow the force field, stopping from time to time to shine his head lamp into it. Though Tim's cyborg implants were more limited than he currently liked, he was able to receive some data from Trac. It helped, though Tim had a feeling the connection was possible because of their proximity.

The force field didn't reflect their light back, or so it seemed to Tim. He had a feeling that there was nothing to see on the other side. At least not as far as their lights penetrated.

And then, after about ten minutes of walking, something

changed. There was a portion of the force field that appeared to be lighter, just ahead of them.

Without voicing agreement to do so, they both quickened their pace.

It was definitely lighter, though the light seemed to be contained by the force field. None of it fell onto the surface they walked on.

Again, nothing he'd ever experienced.

They drew level with it, and as one, turned to face the section of light.

It was filled with a myriad of eyes—eyes like the ones that had examined them while they were in the shuttle. But these eyes weren't huge. They weren't small, like human eyes, maybe the size of his fist.

But so many eyes.

———

Tim sensed something changing underfoot and the light went out. But just before it went out, he thought he saw the eyes vanish.

"We should get back to the shuttle," Tim said. "Something is happening."

"I concur," Trac said. "If you will consent to me carrying you, we can proceed with dispatch."

Tim wanted to say no as emphatically as possible.

"Yes." It was the sensible—if ridiculous—option.

Trac grabbed him and ran. Trac could run very fast. The other thing, Tim noted, was how uncomfortable it was to be carried. None of his cybernetic implants helped with the press of metal to human flesh.

He gritted his teeth. Perhaps he should have asked Trac to let him climb on his back. This under the arm stuff was not optimal.

But they made it back to the shuttle quickly, so his suffering wasn't for long. With his feet back on the surface, it felt as if the disturbance had increased.

And then it didn't just feel, Tim could see something happening. Light was growing at one end of this large containment bay. His suit's sensors picked up on changing pressure. As if this were a large airlock that was depressurizing.

Trac's hold on him changed and Tim realized they'd made it back to the shuttle. Luckily the airlock was still open, but the atmosphere was rushing out.

Trac thrust him into the airlock, despite his protest.

"If necessary, I can hang on to the outside and survive," Trac said.

What he meant was this his chances of survival were greater, but they didn't know what was going to happen.

The hatch closed between them, but Tim couldn't look away from his friend. He knew he'd have secured himself to the outside as well as anyone could have.

It didn't help.

It felt like it took forever for him for the hatch to open at his back and for him to stagger back into the shuttle bay. He spun around and started the cycle for Trac.

The disturbance was increasing. The shuttle rocked with it, setting off a round of murmuring distress from their unwilling passengers.

"You are on board?" Riina's voice was in his ear.

"Yes," he said, his eyes on the controls.

The outer door opened. And then it closed.

Trac was inside.

And then it felt like the bottom fell out of whatever contained them.

Coming into they hadn't sensed anything or felt anything.

This time, he knew the shuttle was falling.

17

Tim grabbed a hand hold, but he still felt himself flailing around. And just when he was sure they'd smash into the ground? Had they been dropped back onto the planet? Or was the thing the aliens had feared happening?

His stomach rose higher in his throat, and the buffeting seemed to increase and then...

It tapered off and they stopped falling with a small bump.

Tim's legs dropped back to the deck with more of a bump than the shuttle.

They were somewhere, but where?

Rinna had hoped they were being returned to the planet, but the sight out of her front view screen did not look anything like the planet they'd been on.

She tried to decide what it was she was actually seeing, it was so chaotic.

As near as she could tell, it was a large space. She craned to peer up out the front view screen and thought she saw stars overhead. No, not stars. Ships. They appeared to be stationary and randomly placed. She had a sense of something vast beyond them, though she couldn't say why.

A soft sound began to filter into the silence, and she realized it was music. For once, there were no words, but the sound fitted their surroundings. The sound of the music was also boundless and terrifying.

But at the same time, it helped her feel grounded. Was it the AI's way of coping?

She pulled her view in from the distant to the particular. Ahead of them was a large chunk of what could have been a spacecraft. And she thought she saw more pieces scattered around.

There was nothing tidy, nothing orderly about the disposition of the debris, but it also didn't look to her as if it had crashed here. It felt more…dumped.

There were patches of sad looking growth on the edges of what could have been a path, but she couldn't be sure.

Her strongest impression was of a drab and bleak place, painted in the dullest of colors, other than the occasional glimpse of a faded logo on the side of a destroyed vessel.

"Veirn?" She wasn't happy to hear the faint quiver in her voice. But it had been a rough day. A long day that didn't look as if it were ending any time soon.

"Our scanning is once again offline," the AI said.

There was an amazing amount of not happy in its tone.

"Is there anyone we can talk to?" Tim asked.

She knew he was casting her worried looks, in between casting worried looks outside.

Then the AI's tone sharpened. "I have locked down all transmissions, both on board and incoming. I believe someone or something is attempting to take control of this ship."

There was sufficient determination in Veirn's voice to tamp down Riina's worry that this might happen. It didn't help with the worry that someone wanted to take control of it. Who or what out there wanted to take over their ship?

"Something is approaching," Trac said. "I believe it is a ground flyer, but not one I've encountered before."

"You don't do a lot of ground missions," Tim pointed out, though absently.

"True," Trac acknowledged, "but I have read your after-mission reports and viewed your video."

"Fair point," Tim said.

The exchange might have made her smile at another time. This was not that time.

Now she could see the approaching flyer, and it was indeed unusual.

Most flyers she'd encountered were aerodynamic in design, so they could move easily through atmosphere with a minimum expenditure of fuel.

This one was wide, flat, blunt-nosed, with a square structure affixed to its surface like an afterthought. Its surface was a patch-work dull as the rest of the place, as if clean and tidy were abhorrent to whoever owned this place.

Its progress was less than smooth as well. It almost seemed to be bouncing its way toward them, but the bounces weren't regular. Its approach was more that of an eager—and ugly—pet.

"That is ugly," Lt. Dish said. "And clunky. It looks like it might crash at any minute."

"Yes," Riina said dryly. "Can we get a read on the outside atmosphere?"

She was starting to have a bad feeling about where they'd landed. The Garradians did not have many waste places. Their goal was always to repurpose as much as possible. And they didn't crash ships very often, at least not in the past.

In this uncomfortable present, they were probably accumulating some damaged ships somewhere. It hadn't been her problem.

It was Trac who was able to take readings. The ship's systems were still on tight lockdown, she noted.

Readings appeared on her screen. Like they'd experienced inside the entity, the readings were a mix of familiar and confusing.

"Are you experiencing any of the attempted intrusions that Veirn is?" she asked. She had almost called them attacks, but that would up the level of concern and it was already pretty high.

"I am," Trac said. "My systems are very robust."

"Do you think they secured any data on us while we were… getting here?" she asked now.

Again, Trac would have been the only one who could have told her, assuming he'd been able to capture readings during their free fall.

"None of their sensing equipment was able to penetrate the outer skin of this shuttle," Trac said.

Garradian ships were also very robust, Riina knew.

The approaching craft had reached them and thumped to landing just shy of the nose of the shuttle.

Rina was aware of a change in Drun's breathing pattern. She wanted to feel sorry for him, but he had wanted to see aliens and now here he was. They could have done without him or his group right now. She was very aware of the extra burden of those lives in this situation.

A ramp jerkily lowered before slamming against a surface she decided was some kind of metal. This was not a natural place, she sensed, despite the dust or dirt cloud that rose around the ramp.

After a fraught pause, a figure began to emerge from inside the craft.

It was large, vaguely humanoid despite its rolls and rolls of what she presumed was flesh. Its feet were naturally huge as well, and slightly splayed as the figure descended. Its clothing was tattered and frayed, not to mention dirty. Trousers rode low on massive hips and when it half turned she saw…

"Plumber's butt," Lt. Dish said. "I wish I could unsee that."

Its shirt didn't cover the ample stomach hanging out over the trousers and said stomach was covered with a mat of dark hair. The figure paused to scratch at this and may have said something because other figure, smaller-in-height figure appeared. He or she was also round with smaller rolls of flesh that even seemed to be settled around the ankles.

The companion's clothes were as shabby and dirty as the larger figure, though thankfully, this figure didn't present a rear view as they both walked toward the shuttle.

The larger figure pulled a large, gray square of what might be fabric out of a pocket and rubbed his glistening face.

His? She studied the face on top of the rolls and decided he did look male. It had a scruffy beard, a partially balding top of his weirdly round head, and a fringe of hair sticking out around the bald spot.

"Well," Lt. Dish said.

When she didn't say anything else, Riina looked back and saw her grimace.

It did seem to sum up the alien's appearance.

The man approached their shuttle and stopped, putting his hands on his ample hips—she presumed they were in their somewhere—and tipped his head back.

His eyes were rheumy, red, and a kind of muddy brown.

He rubbed his face with the cloth again and Riina realized it was illuminated with some kind of light that didn't seem natural.

"Can we hear what he's saying?" Tim asked.

There was a pause. It wasn't a surprise. Veirn was in severe lockdown mode.

Then a voice came through the speaker. She couldn't understand anything but one word.

Garradian.

He had recognized the shuttle. That was interesting, possibly encouraging. Or terrifying. She wasn't sure which.

"I am working on a translation," Veirn said, as if anticipating the question. "Their language is not completely unfamiliar."

Did the AI sound as relieved as this made her feel? It was possibly unreasonable to feel relieved at all. They appeared to have been dropped into an alien dumping depot.

Laws of salvage were different in each system and galaxy. But most laws only went into effect when everyone on board was dead.

That could be good. Or it could be bad. It all depended on the ethics of the two out there.

And they didn't look wildly ethical, not if the gleam of avarice in the big one's eyes were an indication. But looks could be deceiving. Case in point, the former cyborg and the cyborg in their cockpit. First contact with them had been terrifying and fraught.

"I believe I'm beginning to understand them," Veirn said. "They are discussing the salvage of this shuttle and how long it will take to breach its systems."

Sometimes it wasn't wonderful to be correct.

"We will need to talk to them," Riina said.

Tim's head jerked her direction.

"No, I'm not volunteering," she reassured him.

"Humans," Trac said, "could survive in the outside atmosphere, but it would not be comfortable, and they shouldn't stay out there for an extended period of time."

Riina might be relieved to learn this. She should probably be excited about yet another first contact.

She wasn't.

For some reason, perhaps an imp of mischief she didn't know she was capable of, caused her to look at Drun.

He met her gaze, his eyes widening in alarm.

"I can't…" he began.

She took pity on him. "No one thinks you should."

"No one," Tim agreed.

He might have looked affronted at this, but he was too relieved.

"What does our power level look like?" Tim asked.

She was pretty sure he was thinking of the airlock. There was no way they were going to lower the ramp.

But if this went on for too long? What then? The shuttle had some emergency supplies and Harold had come onboard with the supplies he'd taken from the flyers he'd broken into, but how long would it last?

So much depended on just how much trouble they were in.

Tim's head turned. Their eyes met. She didn't know how, but she was sure he shared her thoughts. Her worries.

"Start working with Veirn and," Tim's gaze flicked to Lt. Dish, "the lieutenant in assessing our resources. I will go talk to them."

"I should go," Trac objected.

Tim's gaze went forward, surveying the outside.

"I have a feeling this human shouldn't get a look at you unless we can help it," he said.

"But you," Riina began. He had cyborg implants, visible ones.

"Who else? Do we send Dr. Walker out there? Or one of the Arroxan Prime humans?"

He had a point.

"I don't like it," she said.

"I don't like anything about this situation," Tim said. And then he smiled at her. "So, we have to find a way out of it."

Tim hadn't taken his gear off after his last egress, so he didn't have much to do to get ready. In fact, all he needed to do was secure his head gear.

There were things he wished he could do.

Kiss Riina.

Tell her…it was not the best time to realize that he had strong, unfamiliar feelings for her. Was it love?

He hadn't even known what that meant when his shipmates had used that word.

Love.

Now he might know.

But she didn't know.

And he didn't have time to tell her.

Here he was, going out to try to save their lives, not by breaking things or shooting things—at least not yet. No, he was being tasked with *talking*.

His worst skill

Trac, to his relief, helped him secure his head gear and then slapped him on the back.

The slap knocked him into the bulkhead, but it was the thought that counted. He flexed his shoulder and said, over a feed just between them.

"Take care of Riina."

The robot's gaze met his. He shouldn't have felt or seen emotion there. He wasn't actually sure he did see it. But he knew Trac understood.

This time the slap to his shoulder was restrained. It only knocked him back a couple of steps.

Tim gave his friend a nod. He didn't look back. He couldn't look back and go forward.

Trac opened the hatch. Tim stepped through and it closed behind him. It closed between them.

Riina.

His heart felt tight in his chest. Feelings. These were feelings. He didn't like them. But...without them, he wouldn't know how important this was. He had to save her.

The bay came alive with questions and comments. He ignored them all. The only one not asking was Dr. Walker.

For reasons, Tim didn't understand, Dr. Walker joined Tim at the airlock controls. For some reason the avian was on his shoulder.

Tim looked at it.

"This is T'Korrin," Dr. Walker said, as if that explained everything.

Tim nodded and the bird nodded back. Okay, then, he turned to the hatch control and activated the routine to equalize the pressure.

Dr. Walker waited with Tim until he could step inside, and the hatch closed between them.

Inside, he felt the weight off their expectations, their hopes, their lives, settle on his human shoulders. They'd have been easier to carry without the human body, but...would he have carried them properly? Didn't he need to *know* to do this?

He shifted his shoulders, telling himself that the action spread the weight, made it bearable. And then the hatch opened in front of him and he stepped out.

―――

"I believe I've been able to isolate their jump trail, Captain," Veirn said.

"Enough to follow it?" Kellen rubbed his tired face. It felt like he'd been awake for all of his life. He'd never lost any of his people on a mission before. He didn't like it.

There was a hesitation. It was long enough to make Kellen look up at the camera over his station.

"Veirn?"

"I can't guarantee we will be able to follow it, Captain. It is…a long shot."

Kellen paused, then glanced around his empty bridge. It was him. It was Veirn. If they went home now…

"Let's try," he said. He had to try.

"I agree."

Kellen hadn't asked, but he was glad the AI had said it.

They had to try.

18

Tim stepped out of the airlock onto what felt like some kind of metal plating. It shifted from his weight. He paused to look around.

As a cyborg, he'd been to places like this. Dumping grounds for broken or damaged ships and other equipment. He and the others had visited them in search of parts to repair their ship after encounters with bounty hunters, or just other ships that liked to fight. The ethical nature of the owners of the various dumps was as varied as the types of stock they kept.

But, as robots from the *Najer*, they'd always been treated well. Everyone had been too afraid of them. This alien didn't know them, and he wasn't a robot anymore. So he couldn't scare them into being nice.

Which brought him back to talking. It was definitely ironic.

The airlock wasn't visible from where the two aliens had been, but as Tim turned from his scrutiny of the surroundings, they came around the shuttle, their gazes still on the shuttle.

"I've never seen one of these, just seen specs and heard rumors about them," the big one was saying.

His companion spotted Tim and gave a warning choke that swung the big one's attention his way.

Tim noted that the smaller of the two now had a weapon in his hand, but he hadn't pointed it at Tim yet. It wouldn't take long to lift it, of course, but the little one didn't know he or it wouldn't be fast enough. Tim might not be a robot anymore, but he had enough cybernetics to outpace any non-cyborg.

The larger man studied Tim for a long moment, and Tim wondered what he saw. His cybernetics wouldn't be immediately apparent, though if the alien really focused, he should be able to see his optical device through the transparent faceplate of his head gear.

A smile cut across several folds of the aliens face, but Tim noted it failed to reach the man's eyes.

"I'm afraid this isn't for sale yet," he said.

Tim hesitated. They thought he was a client who had wandered over here? It was data he filed away to think about, mostly because it appeared to indicate a serious lack of security protocols.

"This shuttle will never be for sale," Tim said, finally, watching to see if his words registered. He wasn't certain Veirn was translating correctly.

"And why not?" the big one asked.

"Because I own it. This ship is mine."

"The laws of salvage…"

"Only go into effect when the owner is no longer present," Tim said. It didn't seem wise to use the word "dead," when the little guy was armed. He doubted it could penetrate his Garradian gear, but he didn't know that.

He'd believed the Garradians almost all powerful until he found out they weren't. But their stuff was, according to Colonel Carey of the Earth Expedition, pretty bad ass.

Folds of skin lowered over the big one's eyes, then lifted. Tim didn't like their expression.

"You were on this ship?" he finally asked.

"I was. I am from this ship"

"That could explain why we couldn't…" the little one began but stopped when the big one waved a hand.

"And you never will be able to take it over," Tim said. He'd almost said "we" but managed to stop himself. Don't give any more information than you have to, was a dictum they'd followed well before coming into contact with the Garradians. "I will be leaving soon."

All he needed was his systems back online, navigation information, and a lot of luck.

"The," the word that followed sounded like he barfed, "do not make mistakes in what they bring me."

"Until now," Tim said. "They made a mistake when they… collected my ship and another when they dumped it here."

The big man looked at the shuttle, the longing in his eyes clear for Tim to see, then he returned his attention to Tim.

"I don't think so," he said.

With no warning, the smaller man lifted his weapon and fired.

It impacted solidly against his chest and Tim felt his cybernetics flare to protect him. But the shot did not penetrate the suit.

It hurt some, another side effect of being human, but Tim didn't move. Even as a human, it took more than that to knock him back a step.

He had to admit he longed for his cybernetic body and what he would have been able to do with it. This talking wasn't working that well for him. But…his gut still said that Trac might actually be at a disadvantage here, though he didn't know why.

He kept his own, modest sensors locked down, but felt a kind of buzz against them, as if something were trying to get in.

He and his crewmates' defenses, both physical and systemic,

had been formidable, but there had been a couple of times their systems had almost been breached by viruses.

It had not been optimal to learn they weren't as formidable as they'd believed, too. And they'd worked since then to close that weakness gap. Even as only partly cybernetic, he had those formidable defenses woven into his systems.

He felt the shudder of the decking under his feet. Something, or many somethings, were incoming.

The big one smiled. It wasn't a friendly smile, more one of triumph.

"You should not have left the protection of your ship," he said.

Even as the man spoke, more of the smaller aliens began to appear. All were armed and all of their weapons were pointed at him.

"The law of salvage," Tim tried again.

"There is no law out here," the big one said.

The smaller one might have giggled.

"Do you need backup?" Riina's voice was in his ear.

"No," Tim said. They probably wouldn't need to ask when or if he did need backup. It would be obvious.

He extracted his own weapon but also readied his cybernetics for additional defense. Truth be told, he wasn't exactly sure what they all did yet. He hadn't had time before deploying to test everything. He'd been focused on learning to walk and fight again.

Again, with no warning, the aliens opened fire.

Tim felt the bloom of a protective shield and wondered if it was visible.

It took the impacts, protecting him from the worst of the hits. He still took some, but again, they were mostly annoying.

He didn't fire back. He wasn't sure why. The cyborg Tim would have already leveled them all and moved on. But he'd come out to talk. He needed information as much as he needed not to be killed or captured.

All the shooting paused, and Tim noticed they were making adjustments to their weapons. To up their fire power?

On some level, one not apparent to his conscious mind, he felt the change, and saw the energy wave surge out from him. It passed over most of the aliens firing on him and they cried out and dropped their weapons.

That was interesting. He'd never had that capability as a cyborg. It seemed his Garradian doctors had been tweaking his capabilities. Or CabeX? He felt a certainty as he thought about this captain.

CabeX had been transferred to a human devoid of cybernetics, so it wasn't a surprise he'd try to do all he could to protect his crew.

"What?" The big one finally shouted at him.

Did that mean he was ready to talk? Or was he hoping to stall until more reinforcements arrived? Tim wished he was better at this.

"You can't have my ship," he said. It felt wise to repeat his demand, rather than risk revealing something by talking too much.

He almost grinned at that thought, and what Riina would say if he said he was afraid of it. Talking too much wasn't a *Najer* crew problem.

"I'm going to leave with my ship, in my ship," he added.

"No one leaves here without my permission," the big one said. His tone had a faint edge of a sneer, but Tim had a feeling he was uncertain of his facts.

And then the big one said, now on a whine, "My first Garradian shuttle! Do you know how rare they are? I will buy it from you."

Tim blinked. He'd seen many Garradian ships of all kinds, but even he knew not to say that.

The big man reached out and stroked the side of the shuttle.

"I'll pay whatever you want," he glanced at Tim," within reason, of course."

This seemed like an indication that the big alien was willing to bargain, but other than the ship, Tim had nothing to bargain with.

Information? He couldn't share information about the Garradians with these people.

He gave what he hoped was a contemptuous glance around him.

"I need a ship, not currency," he said.

"I have ships! I have many ships! Come, I will show you!"

If he'd truly been alone on his ship, he'd never have left it. But it felt like a look around might help with their data collection. They were flying blind here.

He gave a sharp nod, one that he hoped gave no quarter in the agreement to look.

"You will withdraw your people," Tim added.

"Of course! Of course!" The big man's hands waved, and the smaller aliens began to retreat.

They could, of course, come back as soon as Tim was out of sight, but Trac was in the shuttle, and his sensors were working.

The big man lead him toward the clunky flyer and Tim followed him inside, his cyborg defenses still fully deployed.

At the place where ramp reached the door, Tim felt a tingle along the edges of his energy barrier and gave mental thanks he was still on his guard.

If the big one was disappointed when Tim continued inside with no sign of distress, he managed to hide most of it.

The big one indicated a seat. Tim shook his head. From the dim recesses of his memory, he recalled being strapped in a chair…

"I'll stand," he said. He had a good chance of breaking free from restraints, but again, not wise to test that right now.

The flyer lifted off with many jerks. Tim rode them easily, but it did explain the erratic course it had flown in coming toward them. He could tell the engine was barely functioning. The big alien maintained his gear as poorly as his junk yard.

He compared what he now saw with their past experiences. They'd only ventured into them as a last resort. There was always the risk that any part they bought would be as damaged as the one they needed to replace. A couple of times, the junk owner had attempted to cash in on the bounty on their heads. They'd learned better, for the most part. Once the owner had insisted on not surviving to learn. CabeX never liked killing and had been angry about it. Not with them but with the fool who had challenged them.

Despite the unappealing looks of both the large and small aliens, Tim felt no desire to end their lives. In his experience, most of those eking out an existence on the fringes of space were either doing their best, or doing what they'd been taught to do

The pilot of the junk flyer steered the craft low over the piles of debris, its screen working well enough for him to see the myriad of broken ships and other space debris, both below and above them. So far, he'd seen no sign of a space capable craft, certainly not one able to go into jump.

What he needed was access to some star charts. He—they needed to know where they were and how to get home.

Their shuttle had some jump capability, but it lacked the star drive that had brought them to Arroxan Prime.

They could now be years or longer, from getting back to Garradian space.

As they flew, Tim heard the big one pointing out some of his prize pieces. As the alien spoke, Tim worked his way carefully into the flyer's systems, looking for usable data.

He had to be so careful. This place was loaded with traps

and hacking devices. His head ached from being under such concentrated attack.

But he also became aware that the alien had not tried to kill him.

He'd tried to capture him.

That was troubling. Did that mean he also dealt in the slave trade? That—and, or possibly or—data mining, were the only two reasons he could think of for them to want to take him alive.

Right now, it was the alienss' hope of securing the shuttle that kept things relatively civil, or so Tim assumed.

He lacked experience. Or did he? He'd observed many interactions of evil men during his years as a slave. Surely, he'd learned something from that time?

With some reluctance, he brought that filter online in his consciousness and began to look for familiar clues.

"None of these craft are space capable," Tim said, hoping for a change of direction. Seeing piles of junk wasn't helpful.

"Right, of course. I just wanted you to know we have the parts, the tech," the big one said.

And he was stalling, hoping something would crack Tim's systems. He turned and looked at the big one, caught him staring at Tim.

The big man started back, his eyes on Tim's face.

Had he finally noticed Tim's cybernetic optical?

"Take us to range four," the big one said.

Tim felt the flyer adjust course, and he added this information into what he was collecting. He would need to be able to find his way back.

It didn't take long, despite the clunky flyer's jerky progress. So, they'd been close to the good stuff, Tim decided. And then he stiffened.

Ahead of him was a *Q'uy* vessel, one not that much unlike the *Najer.*

———

While Tim had been close to the hull, they'd been able to tap into his communications with the aliens. And they'd been able to see the attack.

Riina might be surprised by Tim's moderate response. She had the feeling that Trac was.

"He needs intel," Riina said. "Or we're stuck here."

Trac made a sound that might have been agreement.

Her console pinged with a communication from the bay.

"Yes?"

It was Dr. Walker.

"People are getting a little restless, a little agitated back here."

This wasn't a surprise. They'd been terrified, strapped in and terrified some more, and now they were without input about their current situation.

She wished she knew what their situation was.

She unstrapped and rose, moving to the hatch and opening it.

Faces—white strained faces—turned toward her.

"I expect you are hungry and in need of," she felt her cheeks flush, "private time. We don't have a lot of facilities but what we have, you can use. You'll just need to take turns."

Some of the faces looked relieved at the hope of getting relief. She should have thought of that. But her suit took care of those things while she had it on.

"Dr. Walker and Lira, is it?"

The woman tucked in close to the geologist nodded and for the first time, Riina saw the bird. It was perched on her shoulder. How on earth…?

"It's T'Korrin," Lira said. "He goes where I go."

And then, as if to prove her wrong, it flew into the cockpit. Lira blinked.

"Mostly, he goes where I go." And then she grinned, transforming her face.

So that's why Dr. Walker wants her as his side-chick, Riina thought. She smiled back.

"If you could look at our supplies and distribute some nutrition and hydration packs."

They had about ten people they could have done without. The *Quendala* could have accommodated them easily. It was too late to wish they'd brought the ship into atmosphere instead of the shuttle.

"What is happening?" one woman demanded, though her tone lacked real force. It was more in the range of desperate.

Riina hesitated. She didn't want or need a riot. How much information could she safely give them? She considered them thoughtfully, really looking at them now, and not just seeing them as a bunch of humans who'd come to see aliens.

Well, they'd been brave enough to do that. Perhaps they were brave enough for as much truth as she had.

"We were scooped up by the aliens who were extracting the Vorthari from your planet. We weren't able to communicate well enough with them to stop them leaving the system—your system—with us on board their…ship." Had it been a ship? She still didn't know what the entity had been composed of. "I believe that they dropped us here because they didn't know what to do with us."

"Where is here?" This question came from the one Riina believed was Lira's father.

She faced him. "I have no idea. All our ship's systems but life support were down during the transit. Tim is out there right now trying to get information from the people here."

People? They had been a kind of people. Vaguely humanoid.

"Are they friendly?" Dr. Walker asked.

Riina met his gaze and gave a tiny shake, remembering the sudden one-way fire fight.

"We're not sure what they are," she admitted, feeling he, and they, deserved this much truth. It wasn't much, but then she didn't know much.

She looked around the bay again. They had arms enough for everyone, but not protective gear. If they ended up in another fire fight, there would be casualties.

————

It was ironic, Kellen thought, as they dropped into real space once again, that the element they were following through jump and real space, was something they'd never encountered before.

The thought of it raised the hair on the back of his neck as he had to adjust his thoughts about what it meant to go somewhere he'd never gone before.

There were many places in the Garradian Galaxy he hadn't visited. He'd not been there.

This wasn't that.

He was going somewhere that might not offer a return trip, or a return trip in the lifetime of his colleagues back at Central Command.

He couldn't have done it without Veirn, and he was fully aware how little he was contributing to the actual process. His, um, processing power was no where near that of Veirn's.

Even though he knew he could speak, ask questions, and comment and it wouldn't affect the AI's ability to parse the data, he kept silent. If there was anything for him to know, Veirn would tell him. This required a new level of trust.

It was an uncomfortable level of trust, he could admit to himself. But at some deep level, he knew it was necessary, for him, for Veirn.

Even if it all went wrong, Veirn was doing its best. Kellen knew this, even as his hands clenched and unclenched in his lap.

He should get up and walk around, move his legs and arms. He'd been in this seat for far longer than normal. He was geared up, and his suit accommodated his biological functions. Or it would for a while longer.

Veirn had suggested he don the gear in case of a catastrophic breach in the hull. They were far outside any of the known star maps, traveling with jump drive alternating with the star drive when they could—which wasn't often in completely unknown space.

"You should eat something," Veirn said.

His stomach roiled at the thought.

"My nutritional needs are being met for now," he said. If it went on too much longer, he would have to make adjustments to his suit's systems. But he didn't plan to do that while they were hurtling through unknown space.

"The traces are getting harder to follow," Veirn said.

"I understand," Kellen said. Did he? Possibly he understood. Their mission had always been next to impossible.

For some reason, this made him think of the Earth woman who had married Helfron Giddioni, the former Gadi Leader. Though neither of them had referred to it, Kellen suspected that the interesting Hel was a descendent of his.

And the woman he'd married, that everyone called Doc, had spoken of doing the impossible many times, if others were to be believed. Now he remembered one of her more famous—infamous?—sayings.

"The impossible just takes longer," he said and smiled.

———

The flyer rocked suddenly, viciously. It was more than just a dubious engine and Tim hit the deck, though he was on his feet almost immediately, grabbing onto the back of the seat they'd wanted him to sit in, using it to steady himself.

"What's happening?" he asked.

No one answered. It appeared that the only one strapped in on the flyer was the pilot. The big alien and the smaller alien were both scrambling to get up off the deck. The weight of their, well, weight, was making this almost impossible.

Tim thought about helping them, but they took another hit, and this drove it out of his mind. At their rate, the already unstable integrity of the flyer wouldn't last.

He waited for a moment of relative smooth progress and scrambled to the pilot's side.

"You've got to put down," he said.

"No!" This from the big alien, who had managed to roll over onto his stomach, but might be regretting it. It appeared to concentrate all of his mass in a way that made his arms and legs flail rather than provide thrust.

There was a copilot seat and Tim dropped into it, spiking into the flyer's systems without trying to hide his intrusion this time. It wasn't a smooth transition, unlike their days as robots, but it was a flyer and even if the parts looked different, they did much the same things as ships he was familiar with.

He wrenched control away from the pilot, sighted a clear space and brought the flyer to a jolting, sliding stop that only lightly bumped a ship remnant.

"We will be killed!" The big man yelled.

"A good reason to get out of here," Tim said. He pulled the bigger man, then the smaller man, to their feet and went to the hatch.

"It won't open…"

It opened. When Tim or any of his crewmates, full or partial cyborg, took over a ship, it was thoroughly taken over.

He sprinted down the hatch, not waiting for it to completely lower and dove for cover behind the damaged remains of a smaller craft of some kind.

The others waddled down the ramp, as a row of incoming shots tracked toward the flyer.

"For…" Tim wished he were more familiar with human curse words. He felt the lack as he jumped up, yanked one after the other into cover and dropped down himself, just before the flyer exploded.

During his interface with the ship, he'd managed to download some data, but probably not enough.

He watched as their attacker flew by overhead and wondered if they'd come back for another try.

"We should move," he said. He never liked giving an enemy another chance at a shot at him.

He had to yank them upright again. They were heavy and he'd have failed without his cybernetics. The pilot, Tim noticed, looked impressed.

"This way," that pilot said now and began leading them between the jumbled piles of debris. He couldn't see the *Q'uy* ship now, but he thought he knew what direction it was. But was that knowledge useful? He wasn't sure. If it couldn't fly…

Tim thought he also still knew the way back to the shuttle, but surety would not be possible until he tried and succeeded. Or failed.

He pushed failure out of his mind. He couldn't fail. He had to get back.

"Do you know who attacked?" he asked. He walked beside the pilot, aware of the puffing and panting behind them.

The pilot glanced over his shoulder, then said in a lowered voice, "It's probably Xenmar. This was his depot until Valza took it…over."

Took it from him, Tim guessed. He glanced around. Why would anyone fight over this place?

"I need to get back to my ship," Tim said.

A shadow passed over the surface of the piles of ship parts, and they ducked into cover. Valsa and his side kick weren't quite as fast and were spotted, if the tracery of shots that spurred them into actual speed were any indication.

"That will be difficult," the pilot said. "On foot with Xenmar overhead watching for us. We need transport and that is this direction."

Tim nodded, mulling whether to question the man about their whereabouts in the wider universe. He decided against it for now. They'd been forced to work together. That did not make them friends.

"Wait for us!" The order was imperative, but Valsa lacked the ability to enforce any command.

It was hard for Tim to feel the need to slow down for either of them. At the same time, he had a feeling that Riina wouldn't approve of him just abandoning them to their fate. She had a kinder view than he did. There was also the other fact that he might need the big one at some point, either for knowledge or as a hostage.

Their attacker might trade information and safe passage for him, or Valsa's own people might be held off if they turned out to be hostile, too.

He glanced at the pilot. Or they might just shoot him themselves.

"Where is this transport located? How far away is it?" Tim asked.

The pilot looked away. "It won't be easy to get there." He glanced back again. "Be faster without them."

Tim nodded agreement. No question it would be easier and faster.

"But we might need him," Tim said, not looking at the pilot.

When the pilot didn't speak, Tim did look in his direction. He nodded thoughtfully.

"He's got to be the worst hostage ever though," the pilot said.

It was a truth that Tim couldn't argue with.

"The smaller guy is armed." Tim looked back again. Both men were visibly puffing and panting.

"We should take it away from him."

"Yes," Tim said, but he was looking around. They needed a way to keep the two moving, or they wouldn't be worth the risk. "If you can, get it."

"What are you going to do?"

"Find a way to transport them. They are slowing us down."

19

"Something's changed."

Riina looked at Trac, then down at the consoles in front of her.

Their ship's status go lights were coming on.

"Our systems are coming back online," she said, not even trying to hide her relief. "When can we get in the air?"

They needed to get back into contact with Tim. She needed to see Tim with her eyes and not just sensors, though it was a relief to see his tracking device show up on her screen again.

"What's that?" Lt. Dish said.

Riina looked up and back, saw the lieutenant was pointing outside and turned to look.

"Someone," Trac said, "is firing at Tim's location. Or close to his location."

"We need to get in the air now," Riina said, knew she did a poor job of muting her sense of urgency.

"Are you sure…" Drun began.

Riina cut him off. "I'm very sure." She turned to Trac. "Get us airborne. I'm going to change."

Trac met her eyes. His blank gaze still managed to convey that he wasn't happy.

"I should…" he began.

"You have to protect the ship and our passengers," she said. "We'll need a ride out of here."

All they needed was a route. She stared at the flashes coming from the vessel that now showed up on their tracking.

"Tim is very tough," Trac said, "despite…"

He didn't finish his sentence. He didn't have to. Riina knew his humanity made him vulnerable in a way that was new to them both.

"He needs me to have his back," she said. "Is our cloak working?" At Trac's nod, she added, "I'll gear up, and you can drop me near his location."

"Do you wish me to engage with the intruder?"

Riina hesitated. She wanted him to blow it out of the sky but, "We don't know who the good guys are or if there are any good guys out there."

They might need that ship's help. Or its databanks. Be a pity to blow it out of the sky and then find out they could have used it.

This time, when Trac answered her, it was on a private comm. It was better that Drun didn't know everything they were thinking. He might panic. Or try to stop them, though she didn't see how he could manage that.

She wished he'd go back with his people in the bay. She couldn't quite tell where and how he fit into their command structure. If there was one. They all appeared to be civilians except for Drun.

But Drun hadn't overtly taken the leadership role until he'd demanded to join them in the cockpit. But had that been a leadership move? Or a power move? An annoying move? It could have been that.

Riina ignored him now, heading for the bay. Back inside, she was aware of all of them watching her change out of her regular gear and don what she'd never worn before.

Assault gear.

She knew, without being told, that their passengers were growing unsettled as she strapped on weapons and checked her various suit's levels.

She was bluffing. Oh, she knew how to put it on. It was part of her training. She even knew how to point and shoot. She just hadn't done it before.

She dropped her faceplate, so that when she turned to face them, they wouldn't see her fear, her uncertainty. The only thing that kept her going was knowing that Tim was out there alone, with enemies on every side.

They were a team. She should never have let him go out there alone. She would not make that mistake again.

Her suit's comm activated.

"Cloaked and lifting off now," Trac said.

———

"I have picked up the trail again," Veirn said. "I believe they made a stop in this system. That increased the levels of the element I am using to track them."

"Do we have any information on this system?" he asked.

"Nothing that would indicate why they stopped here," Veirn said. "It is curious because it is, or was, within range of one of the older outposts, but that outpost went out of service."

Kellen checked the data Veirn displayed on his console. It had gone down while they were all still in their long sleep. Had it been destroyed? It could have been either malicious or natural.

Many of the outposts had been damaged by space debris of one kind or another.

However, it was odd that there was no data previous to when it went offline. That seemed to indicate deliberate destruction.

"I am detecting life signs on one of the planets." There was a pause, then Veirn added, "It is an inhabited planet, not a minor incursion."

So, the entity had stopped here? Kellen frowned.

"No sign of the electro-magnetic interference that Arroxan Prime experienced?"

"No sign," Veirn confirmed. "Previous data on the planet had no inhabitants detected."

"If they destroyed the outpost," Kellen said, "to hide their colonization…"

He didn't, he couldn't quite finish the thought, as he was unsure where he wanted—or didn't want—to go with it.

They could have simply perceived the outpost as hostile.

Or they'd had something to hide.

Whatever their reason for possibly destroying the outpost, it all indicated that they were interstellar. They might be capable of launching an attack on the *Quendala*.

"We don't have time to find out," Kellen said, though reluctantly. If they were hostile, he didn't like the idea that they were behind them. And if they weren't hostile? They could be paranoid. Also didn't like that behind them.

He checked. They were cloaked. So hopefully their passage through this system would go undetected.

"Let's leave a sensor drone behind," he said. He recalled Doc also saying something about protecting your six.

———

Tim was pleased that the big one and his smaller friend had taken shelter in the remains of a ship. It allowed whoever was shooting at them to concentrate their fire. It was in hopes of this outcome that he'd refrained from shooting back at the attacker.

And the fact that he felt some sympathy with the attacker.

This left him and his pilot companion somewhat free to find the ship that the pilot claimed was here.

Tim wasn't entirely happy about working with the pilot. Riina would have said, "Trust issues."

It was true he had many and for good reason. But he missed her at his side, watching his back.

It was much harder to both monitor the attacker and keep an eye on the pilot while in this human body. And he realized he'd missed something.

The constant attack against his cybernetics, against his internal systems, was gone. It had been a buzz against his skin. It wasn't so much that he lacked the necessary inputs for so small a task. It was that he hadn't thought about it.

He didn't like that. Was it a failure of his human body or his imagination? In any case, it was a failure.

His comms crackled for the first time since he'd flown away with the big alien.

Did the viral attack going down also mean that the shuttle was able to come back online? It seemed so when he heard Trac's voice over his comms.

"We are lifting off and will proceed to your location. Try not to die before we get there."

One couldn't accuse Trac of being overly sentimental.

"I will endeavor to remain alive," he said. He might not need the alternative transportation, but he didn't tell his pilot friend that. He preferred the arrival of backup to remain a secret for as long as possible.

Even if the shuttle could retrieve him, they had no way to leave without navigation data. He was going to have to find a way to—as Doc liked to put it—get down and dirty with some databanks. He'd have been happier about that if he weren't half human.

————

Riina was waiting for the airlock pressure to equalize, so she could step inside when Harold, Dr. Walker's robot friend approached her.

It didn't speak out loud, but it instead initiated a private connection with her.

With equal parts curiosity and impatience, she accepted the connection.

"I would like to proceed with you," it said.

She looked it up, then down. It wasn't a heavily armed robot, but it did have some basic defenses. She knew its specifications. Knew these defenses were why it had been assigned to Dr. Walker.

She hesitated. It might be useful, but it might also be needed here. Trac could handle himself very well, but if their passengers got antsy and started causing trouble, even he might have a hard time piloting and doing crowd control.

She transmitted these concerns and watched the robot's eyes flicker as it processed her response.

"We need to access databanks to find our way back, do we not?" It asked.

She nodded. "But Tim…"

"Tim is not fully cybernetic, and you might be taking fire."

It had a point.

"How about this. I drop down and help Tim secure his situation. You scan for databanks now that the interference is gone. And if needed, you can join us."

"That is a reasonable alternative."

Riina blinked. Did the robot sound disappointed?

"I appreciate the offer." She did. As far as she knew, the robot hadn't been programmed to take dangerous risks.

The other reality was that the airlock only held one at a time and Trac would have to linger in the area to also allow the robot to join them.

"I really do appreciate your offer," she said again, "and we will probably need you, so it's better not to get you shot up by exposing you early."

"That is fair," the robot said. "And also reasonable."

It did sound happier, which it should whether it was sentient or not. She'd worry about any robot that was eager to get shot at.

She was kind of worried about herself.

She heard a squawk and looked down. The bird, T'Korrin had apparently followed her out of the cockpit. Now the bird ruffled its feathers and shifted from foot to foot.

"T'Korrin wants to go with you," Lira said.

Rinna looked at her, aware that Lira couldn't see her incredulous expression. She kind of wanted both of them to see it, but she didn't lift her faceplate. She looked down at the bird. It ruffled its feathers again.

"Why?" Riina asked.

Lira shrugged. "I have no clue. But whenever I've not done what he wanted, I've been sorry."

Riina bit back a sigh. "When Harold comes down, T'Korrin can come with him?"

She made it a question, even though it wasn't one.

Lira looked at the bird. It looked back and appeared to shake its head. Riina almost gave in, but she was dropping into a fire fight.

"Deal with it, T'Korrin," Lira said.

The airlock signaled pressure balanced. Her last view of the bird was of it shaking its head from side to side. She opened the hatch and slid inside. It was small and she marveled that Tim had managed to get his shoulders inside.

He had wide shoulders. She sighed, recalling those shoulders as the air hissed out.

———

Tim had told the pilot he would keep watch, while the man tried to access the ship he claimed would fly. He'd prefer that pilot be distracted when the shuttle arrived. It was cloaked, and his human eyes couldn't see it, but his cybernetics registered the shuttle's proximity.

The ship that the pilot considered flight-worthy looked like a piece of junk to Tim, but if it kept the man busy, he was content.

That didn't mean he took his sensors off him. He had a small video of his movements on a floating screen using his cybernetic eye. The man moved, as if to block visuals, so Tim deployed a small drone to keep on eye on him.

The man could just be trying to get away and planned to leave him behind. Tim might have understood that imperative more, if they weren't so desperately in need of data.

His suit registered the shuttle overhead and he transferred the bulk of his attention up. He didn't see the airlock open.

He did see a figure step out, dropping down toward him. He waited tensely for the flare of rockets that would slow her descent.

They didn't…she'd waited until she was below the level of the debris he was hiding behind, he realized when they finally flared.

He understood why she'd done it, but he still wanted to shake her for scaring him.

Her gear could probably have absorbed some of the impact

of a forceful landing, but it would have caused her pain and possible injury.

As soon as she'd touched down, she crouched and scanned for his location.

He signaled to her, then had his attention yanked away from her by something he saw on his drone camera.

The pilot had accessed the ship. And was now closing the hatch behind him.

It was so disappointing when humans lived down to your expectations.

20

Rinna pulled her hand weapon, saw Tim signaling to her, and in a crouching run, made it to his side without getting shot at.

His free hand—the one not holding a weapon—found and crushed her hand in greeting. She didn't dare look at him. She couldn't afford to be distracted from assessing her surroundings.

The landscape had been intimidating viewed from inside the shuttle. Here on the ground? It might be terrifying if she allowed herself to think about it too much.

The tumbled remains of damaged ships and other, harder to identify debris, made it more hellscape than landscape.

Rust, fire damage, weapons impacts, and neglect had all made themselves felt in everything she could see. A hellscape certainly suited the doughy alien she'd watched waddle importantly down his barely functioning flyer ramp.

What was it about this place that made the man feel important? She'd have been embarrassed for this to be her domain.

She had a sense of movement at her feet and glanced down. She managed to stifle the scream down to a gasp—helped by the fact that the large insect hadn't stopped as it passed her by.

The somewhat larger—and harder to classify—animal that seemed to be after it, also didn't look at her.

This time she choked because she'd been in the process of gasping when she saw it and they were incompatible sounds.

"What's wrong?" Tim asked.

"I guess I shouldn't be surprised that this place has a vermin problem," she said, trying and mostly succeeding in giving him a smile. And then, when he looked surprised, her smile deepened into something without the strain. "You hadn't noticed?"

"I'm not accustomed to interacting with vermin," he admitted.

Now he looked around him. Of course, there was nothing vermin-like in view but he managed to not look skeptical. She almost thanked him but realized he'd have no clue why. They had enough on their problem plate without adding male and female interactions to the list.

"He seems to be keeping his head down," Tim said, his attention turning back to the place where the ship still fired on a position. "Or he's dead."

"Is that where the large alien is? Did you want him to not be dead?" Riina asked. She guessed it had to be where the doughy alien was hiding, since he wasn't in their vicinity.

"He might be a bargaining chip," Tim said.

That was a very large "might," Riina decided. He was a very dirty—and as previously noted—doughy chip. On the other hand, whoever was in the hostile ship seemed determined to take him out. But could they, in good conscience, trade his life for theirs?

She would have been a decided no on that subject, but it wasn't just their lives. The shuttle also contained their mostly unwilling passengers. That turned a slightly difficult right and wrong equation into something much more complex.

How many lives saved were worth one, rather nasty life? She'd never had to face these questions before the long sleep.

That wasn't because complex moral questions weren't there, just that her contact with them had been limited.

In other words, not her job.

Now here she was, in some unknown junkyard, fully armed, and…what?

"If we save his life," she said, "will that help us get out of here?"

She didn't say it out loud, but she hoped the meaning was clear to Tim. If they got involved in the current…quarrel…was there any benefit to them?

They didn't have to help him get killed or save him from being killed. She still felt a distinct qualm. She knew this was dancing on the head of a moral pin. But they also weren't positioned to even help themselves at the moment.

"We couldn't afford to tell him we're lost," Tim said, his tone matter-of-fact.

It was interesting that Tim was so good at seeing and understanding the motives of bad people, and so lost where it came to, well, women. Though, probably not a surprise. He'd spent his formative years with bad people.

She wasn't sure why her senses all of a sudden went on the alert—even before she received a warning signal from Trac. And before the low, menacing growl from behind them.

She put a hand on Tim's arm, turning with him to face…

It was large. It was canine, judging by the teeth currently bared at them. The teeth were huge and looked sharp, though maybe it was the dripping saliva making them glisten and look sharp.

More shapes emerged out of the shadows. At least six of the canines.

"Of course there'd be junkyard dogs," Lt. Dish said over the comms.

Tim pulled her next to him, so that their backs were against a large ship. She wasn't sure it helped their situation that much when a large string of saliva dropped at their feet from above.

She risked a look up. Why yes, there was one of the canines up there, too. She was pretty sure she counted six—that they could see.

At least, she thought somewhat distantly, she probably wouldn't have to make a decision about whether to save that doughy alien. They'd be fortunate to save themselves.

———

"If this situation weren't so crappy," Tim heard Lt. Dish say over the comm, "it would almost be hilarious, it is such a cliché."

Tim ignored her interjection. It wasn't relevant that he could tell. His sensors had found at least eight of the canine creatures, with other stealthy movement that might indicate more of them closing on their position.

It would have been ridiculously easy to deal with them if he weren't half human. And if Riina weren't here? He might have found it, not easy, but manageable.

"You shouldn't have come," he said, shifting so that she was mostly behind him.

"Probably not," she agreed.

She didn't sound upset. He didn't dare look to see if she was upset.

The canines were pacing slowly closer, their tails snapping from side to side. He had the sense they were trying to discover how well armed they were.

His initial thought—to boost Riina up on the ship at their backs—had, of necessity, been abandoned. These predators had done a good job of cutting off all retreat.

He wondered how sentient they were or if they were acting on instinct.

He shifted again, so that Riina was fully behind him. He

released the longer weapon strapped to his back. He could operate both, but he was looking for the best, first target.

If these were canines, if they had canine instincts, then there might be an alpha, a leader. He wanted to target that one.

His sensors noted and cataloged the canines in each position, comparing size and other factors.

"I think that one's in charge," Riina said. "The one in the center. Typical pack behavior," she added.

His own calculations had determined the same thing, but he had to smile that she'd done it using her eyes and from behind him.

And then the smile faded as he braced, noting that the leader was bunching for an attack. Tim aimed, but before he could trigger his weapon, there was a roar of motion overhead, like a burst of wind passing overhead.

He didn't take his eyes off the pack. He didn't dare, but his other sensors noted—with considerable surprise—that it wasn't the shuttle, but the ship that the flyer pilot had entered.

Was he trying to help them? Or just passing by?

The canine pack retreated some, as if they were also uncertain.

He felt Riina's hand on his shoulder as she said softly, "What if there were other energy barriers in different locations? When they went down, these canines were able to enter areas that had been blocked off to them?"

Tim wasn't sure why it mattered.

Tim had bare warning, just long enough to turn and protect Riina, before the ground between them and the canines exploded, dirt and debris rising in the air.

He thought he saw a few bodies flying, too. Tim had a sense of something larger in the air—something with wings—but that's all he had time for.

The ship that had fired the shot lurched once, then went spinning out of sight, its engines screaming from the attempt to recover from the impact. At least the pilot had tried to help. Or shoot them himself. Tim wasn't entirely sure.

"You're still cloaked, right?" Tim muttered into the comms.

"Affirmative," Trac said.

"What is it?" Riina asked.

"It is a large avian," Trac said.

"I did not have *Jurassic Park* on my bingo card," Lt. Dish said.

The debris cloud began to settle, but it was Tim's sensors that registered the remaining canine's slinking back into the shadows.

The large avian settled into the clearing left by the explosion. If Tim hoped it hadn't seen them, it was a faint hope. The avian was facing them, the slow movement of its wings brushing against the ground and reaching to both sides of the tumble of debris.

Its red eyes regarded them from either side of a beak that looked like it could peck through metal.

The ground underfoot rumbled slightly. From the ship's impact with the surface, Tim guessed. He hoped the pilot managed a controlled crash. It did appear he had tried to help them.

The other ship, the one that had been firing on the big alien was nowhere in sight, nor was it visible on his sensors.

————

The silence from Veirn began to tell on Kellen. If asked, he'd have said he had no problem traveling without other humans on his ship.

It wasn't about that, he told himself. It was about his missing humans. And the lack of input from the AI. Humans, he reminded himself, needed input, they needed data—or the pretense of data.

And he missed—he half frowned—the sense of sharing the worry perhaps? That could be it.

He felt useless. All he could do at present was worry. He'd resisted the temptation to break the silence. He knew Veirn would inform him if there was anything to tell him. He knew this.

The AI wasn't like a human who talked to hide their worry. It just didn't talk unless it had something to say.

The words, the questions, the worry felt thick in his throat, as if he needed to cough them up to breath freely again.

"How are we doing?" he asked, finally, when he could hold them back no more.

"The data is interesting," Veirn said, surprising Kellen.

Had it been hoping for a conversation, too?

"The level of the element changes. Based on previous observations, I believe it changes as they are going in and out of jump. I'm starting to collect enough data to postulate that it also changes based on duration out of jump."

"So, they stopped in some places longer than others?" He was pretty sure that's what Veirn was saying, but it didn't hurt to ask.

"I believe so."

The confirmation didn't help that much, since they didn't know why the entity was stopping anywhere.

"I believe we are approaching another drop out point," Veirn said. "The element is occurring in more density than previous stops, however."

"That's…curious," Kellen said, resisting the urge to ask Veirn what it meant. It couldn't know and it would just have to smack him down.

"Indeed," Veirn said. "I have noticed our ships, when breaking heavily, leave expanded element debris. It is possible, they—how do the Earth humans put it—slammed on the brakes."

"Then we should probably follow suit," Kellen suggested.

"I agree," Veirn said.

———

Rinna appreciated Tim's efforts to protect her, but it was also annoying not to be able to see what was happening.

A large avian.

A little helpful but lacking a lot of specifics.

She tried to peer over Tim's shoulder. She couldn't. So she crouched down and tried to look under his arm.

It was a little better. A little.

She crouched some more and then wished she hadn't.

A large avian was *so* lacking in specifics. Yes, it was large, almost as big as the shuttle, she decided, based on where the top of its head reached against the damaged ships on either side.

It had black, gray, and dirty white coloring. A beak that—if clean—might be orange. Instead, it was a dingy brown. The only real color were its eyes, which were red with gold centers.

It had beefy legs, and a claw span that looked impressive this far away. She hoped she wasn't going to find out how impressive. She realized it had some kind of electronic device secured around one leg, and she wondered who had been brave enough to do that.

It lifted its head, extending its neck, its wings flapping and gave a sound that sent chills snaking down her back.

She hoped, she really, really hoped, it wasn't calling to more of its kind. That it had scattered the canines was only a minor positive.

"We're in so much trouble," she muttered, not sure who was hearing her. Or if anyone was. She couldn't move to check her comms or move to do anything.

"Yes," Tim said.

Its claws scrapped against the surface, cutting through the

debris to the metal base as it took a couple of steps closer, its head lowering to regard them.

She had the feeling it was hoping they'd do something. Perhaps its eyes needed movement? Or it wanted an indication of intent?

It was also curious—a side thought to perhaps reduce her rising tension—that there was metal under foot. What was this place? Other than Lt. Dish's junkyard?

Its head tipped to one side, bringing up a memory of before, when she lived planet-side with regular sized birds. Just so did they look at a worm before stabbing at it.

It had been cuter on the smaller bird.

But...was there a kind of intelligence in the eyes? They'd encountered sentient animals, quite a lot of them recently. Was this one?

And again, her mind circled back to the question: what was it and what was it doing here?

It made another sound, a smaller one this time. Was it hope that made her catalog it as less hostile? Delusion?

And then, amazingly, she heard another bird sound. A smaller bird, well, small compared to the large avian, flew past it and landed on Tim's shoulder.

It was T'Korrin. And yes, it gave her a pointed look before directing its attention toward the avian.

It settled firmly, its claws digging into Tim's suit shoulder until it seemed satisfied. And then it began to squawk. Make avian sounds anyway.

It paused, as if waiting, and then started again, the sounds slightly different from before.

"I'm kind of terrified," Riina said, quietly into her comm.

"Lira," Lt. Dish said, "thinks T'Korrin can help."

Riina wanted to ask the usual questions, where, why, how, what the freaking heck—that Earth phrase felt right for the occasion.

She didn't.

The large avian's head tipped the other direction. Its wings shifted, lifting just a bit before settling down again.

And finally, it made a small sound.

———

Riina, Tim was somewhat relieved to realize, was staying calm. He could only be somewhat relieved because he expected the avian to attack at any moment.

He was not happy that the stowaway bird called T'Korrin was trying to communicate with the large avian.

It could fly away if it went wrong.

Still, the large avian hadn't attacked yet.

Yet.

He had inputs. He had sensors. He should have known where everyone was—friend and foe—and what was happening around him. Perhaps it was a function of being human that he was so hyper focused on the big bird and unable to process anything else.

It was somewhat comforting to feel Riina pressed against his back. If he was going to die—he found himself unable to complete the thought. He didn't want her to die, too, even though he also didn't want to die alone.

He wanted…he wanted them both to live. To walk away together from this. But if they were to die, he needed to tell her…

"Rinna." Somehow he managed to secure a private connection with her, despite his frozen inputs and outputs.

"Yes."

"I, you need to know," he had to swallow. Curse his human throat, his human brain that struggled to find the correct words, if that were possible.

"Yes?" Her voice was gentle.

There was no way for him to truly feel her through their suits, but he was still sure that somehow she'd softened and pressed closer.

"I do not understand all the words or feelings, but I believe, based on what I have seen with the others, that I…" for a moment the word caught in his throat. He forced it out. She deserved it. "I love you. I believe I love you."

"Oh, Tim."

The softness in her voice, the happiness closed his throat with something thick. How could she sound happy in their current situation?

"I love you, too."

The surge of joy caught him by surprise. So that was how it worked. They were going to die. Probably. And they were happy.

"I wish…" He wished he could turn around and take her in his arms.

"I know," she said. Her hands left his shoulders and slid around his waist.

His suit registered contact the length of his back and legs. His body registered, well, something else.

She loved him. He didn't want to die, but at least he could die happy. Yes, it was happy, though strange and unfamiliar to one who had been content to be free. He'd thought it was enough. He was glad he'd had the chance to feel this before he died.

And he wished one of them spoke avian.

T'Korrin hopped off his shoulder and trotted over to the big avian, passing under its formidable beak without problem. He reached the big bird's leg and Tim realized, for the first time, that it had an electronic device circling its beefy leg.

T'Korrin tapped it, then looked back at Tim and chirped at him, its head angling as if to say, "Come get this off."

"Tim," Rinna's voice held a warning note.

He holstered his hand weapon and handed her his long weapon. "Hold this," he said.

"Tim," she said again.

"It will be fine," he said. "Cover me without looking like you're covering me," he added.

"Right," she said.

He thought he heard irony in her tone and might have smiled in other circumstances. In this one, he paced carefully forward, his hands in clear sight. The large avian watched, its head lowering as he drew closer.

He passed within inches of that deadly beak and half expected it to stab into his back and he stepped under the body. He stopped by the leg, then knelt down and studied the device.

"You seeing this?" he said, in his comm.

"Most curious," Trac said.

"Curious good or curious bad?" Tim asked. He cautiously touched it, his fingers sliding along a surface that appeared to be smooth.

"I'm not sure yet. Zoom in on that section," Trac said suddenly.

Tim did as requested, also focusing his human thoughts on the spot. It was the only place that wasn't perfectly smooth.

"I think there is a port here," Tim said, finally. He touched the small indentation with the tip of his finger. He extended an access cable toward it, half expecting to get a jolt from it, but it slid in. After the obligatory "handshake," he started sensing data. "I can't read it," he said to Trac.

"Veirn's fragment is attempting to translate it," Trac said. "But I am assuming that the goal is to remove the device?"

"That is my belief," Tim said.

"Based on my experience with similar devices, a surge of power should do the job."

Or hurt the avian, Tim thought ruefully. And make it mad while he was kneeling inches from its claws.

"I think the canines are coming back," Riina said, "using the high ground."

Tim checked. She was correct. Their heat signatures were moving across the surface of the debris that circled them.

"Faint heart," said Lt. Dish, "never won fair lady."

He looked up, where he imagined the ship to be. "What?"

"Just do it," Trac said.

It wasn't Tim's imagination that there was humor in his tone. Easy for him.

He sent the surge, without a countdown. If he stopped to think, his heart would be faint.

A small puff of smoke emerged from the device. There was a click and it fell off at Tim's feet.

"Androcles and the Lion," Lt. Dish said, now.

This time he didn't ask what. He waited. The air came alive as the big bird's wings moved, sweeping the area with a wind that swirled the dirt, then it lifted off, the force of it almost knocking him onto his back.

He instinctively covered his head as the legs and claws brushed his shoulder. The ground debris seemed to rise, too, swirling like a small storm. The avian cried out as one of the canines leapt from its perch and landed on its back.

The other canines tried to join the attack, but the avian was rising too quickly. Several fell, landing not far from Tim. T'Korrin rose, crying out as Tim spun to face this new attack. His hand weapon was pulled and his back toward Riina.

One of the canines howled, shifting as if in pain, then rolled to its feet and barred its teeth at him. But as it paced toward him, it showed signs of injury. Two of the canines moved feebly, more seriously injured he concluded.

He reached Riina, took the long weapon she held out, noted that she then deployed her weapons as well. He felt an odd reluctance to further injure the canine, which made no sense.

"We don't want to hurt you," Riina said, at his side.

He didn't look at her, though he wanted to. Had she picked up on his reluctance, or did it come from some place inside her.

"Why?" he asked.

"They are probably prisoners here, too," she said.

And then he got it. They weren't so unlike, he and the other crew of the *Najer*. Trapped by circumstance. Dangerous by necessity. Angry and frustrated. As he now looked at them, others had stared at him and the others as they were forced to attack. How he'd hated it.

"No," he said. "I don't want to hurt you."

The canine stopped, his head tipping to one side, as if considering what he'd said. Was that even possible?

It lifted its head in a long, mournful howl and then turned and disappeared back into the shadows. His sensors showed the other canines following suit.

T'Korrin dropped down, landing on his shoulder again and made a sound that was almost approving, or so it seemed to him.

"Thank you, T'Korrin," Riina said. "I'm sorry I didn't listen to you before."

T'Korrin made a huffing sound, then hopped onto her shoulder and rubbed the side of her head.

"I hope that means I'm forgiven," she said.

T'Korrin chirped again, then lifted off as the empty center once more swirled into a small storm around an invisible object.

Trac was bringing the shuttle in to collect them.

21

_____

"What is it?" Kellen asked, as the ship's sensors found a large, apparently solid object in the swirling mass of the cosmic cloud.

"The readings are unusual," Veirn said. "But the element trail leads directly to it."

"Does it also lead away from it?" Kellen frowned, wondering if the entity had stopped here for long and why? This region of space had little to recommend it. No close planets. Debris and asteroid fields. The cosmic cloud. Only a very distant sun.

"Yes, it does," Veirn said, "but we need to be sure our people aren't here before we move on."

It was correct, and Kellen felt something stir inside at Veirn's words.

Our people.

The AI had risked as much or more than any of them in trying to find their people. If he had wondered if it was sentient? He didn't now. He wished he knew how to tell the AI this.

"We might have a problem, Captain," Veirn said. "But there is some good news."

Hadn't one of the Earth people said something about good news and bad news? And how to receive it?

"Let's start with the good news," he said, and then was sure he'd got the order wrong.

"I'm picking up a signal from the shuttle."

Well, that was good news.

"And the bad news?"

"There is a small fleet of ships between us and the shuttle's location. It's coming from that unknown solid object," Veirn added.

"A blockade?"

"If it looks like a blockade," Veirn said. "And blocks like a blockade…"

"It probably is a blockade," Kellen said. "But why? What's there?" Besides their shuttle? he added to himself. But what kind of draw was it?

————

They had clear access to the shuttle, but they still lacked the information they needed to get home.

"You go first," Tim said. "I'll cover you and T'Korrin."

But before Riina could move, the large avian reappeared, dropping down almost like a stone and landing on top of the shuttle. It was a strange sight, since the shuttle was still cloaked. It looked like the bird was perched in midair. She'd have smiled, except for the fact that the large bird was now sitting on their ride.

"Who let the dogs out," Lt. Dish said, "or rather, who brought them back?"

They were indeed back and making no effort to hide.

"My mom used to say that no good deed ever went unpunished," Lt. Dish added.

It might be the first time Riina understood something Lt. Dish said.

The canines, the dogs as Lt Dish called them, crouched on their haunches, not in attack positions. That seemed like a small positive. The avian settled in like a bird on a perch, its wings tucked in at its sides.

T'Korrin flew up, once more facing the larger avian on its perch. Riina studied them. It almost looked like they were chatting.

"The other ship is back," Tim said.

"I confirm that," Trac said.

"What's it doing?" Riina said.

"Circling this location, but at a safe distance," Trac said.

Was there such a thing?

"Has anyone seen our host recently?" Riina asked.

"I've been keeping an eye on him," Lt. Dish said.

She had? She exchanged a surprised look with Tim.

"He and his little friend," a note of irony crept into her voice, "are still hiding in that derelict, or what's left of it. It took a lot of incoming. So, they might be…"

She didn't finish the thought.

"We need to check it out," Tim said.

Riina nodded. They still needed someone with star chart data. At the moment, he was their only option.

"I could check it out," Trac offered.

To her surprise, Tim shook his head.

"There is a damaged *Q'uy* ship here," he said, as if that explained everything.

And perhaps it did. The presence of the ship could mean that the doughy alien was also familiar with the *Q'uy* robots.

"There was an energy field and other protections in place here until…" Tim paused. "Something took them down. But they could have been designed for my kind, before we, well, before," Tim finished.

Riina knew some about before, knew more about after. She knew what had been done to upgrade their virus protections and other things. She knew how close a virus had come to taking them down. Had this place been rigged with them? It sounded as if that was what Tim was implying.

Veirn's fragment had talked about something attacking the ship.

"Trac definitely needs to stay on the shuttle," she agreed. There could be more traps, a trap designed specifically for someone like Trac. "You have good instincts," she told Tim.

He looked surprised. "I do."

"It's part of being human," she told him and his look of surprise deepened. He was, she realized, still working on that human part of himself. "It's a work in progress for all of us."

———

"Timmy's in the well," Lt. Dish said, over the comms.

Tim was too startled to even blink. Luckily Riina spoke what he was thinking.

"What?"

"It's, well, *Lassie*, but you wouldn't know that." Lt. Dish, stopped, "it's a kind of Earth shorthand for someone needing help."

If someone needed help that the huge avian couldn't handle? Tim wasn't sure they could.

Riina met his gaze and shrugged. "At this point, anything is possible." She stepped closer to the cloaked shuttle and looked up.

"T'Korrin, does someone need our help?"

She was asking the *bird*. He opened his mouth to point out that what they needed were star charts, flight data, a path home. But T'Korrin's wings lifted, half lifting it off its perch.

"Is that yes?" he asked, dubiously.

"I think it might be," Riina said.

Tim thought about asking if Lira could join them, but he had a feeling that would include Dr. Walker. That exposed too many humans to risk. He wished he could persuade Riina to go back inside the shuttle.

"Okay," Tim said, "how about this." He couldn't believe he was talking to a bird, or possibly two birds. "We go see what we can do to help…whoever. You lift, Trac, and see if you can find some kind of central control for this place. I have a feeling there is more we need to know."

"There is always more we need to know," Trac said, "but if you can get the avian to get off, I will go see what I can do."

"Just don't get out of the shuttle to do it," Tim cautioned. All they needed to turn this from a Charlie Foxtrot—Earth for messed up, he understood—to a major catastrophe was for Trac to get taken over and turned against them.

"I'll keep an eye on him," Lt. Dish said.

"Thank you," Riina said, when Tim didn't respond.

He couldn't respond. Because if he did, he would say, "It needed only that." So, he didn't.

"Which way?" he asked instead.

The large avian lifted off the shuttle. So did T'Korrin. The avian landed on the debris to their right.

"You can go," Tim said. He'd feel better with the shuttle in the clear. Better? Well, less awful.

When the shuttle had lifted away, stirring up more of the nasty dust, Tim took a moment to be grateful for his suit's filters that made it possible for him to *not* smell that stirred up air.

Before he could do more than think this, the avian had dropped back into the vacated space.

"Weren't we just here?" Riina asked.

T'Korrin flew down and landed on the avian's head. Then he waved his wings and danced from one foot to the other.

"He doesn't, he couldn't want us to…" Riina's voice trailed off as the large avian lowered its head and angled its body.

"I think he does," Tim said.

"Well," Riina said, "we did say we'd help."

She started forward, but Tim caught her arm.

"I'll go first," he said. If this was a trick, she'd have some warning to get away while he got pecked to death.

But the avian didn't peck him. It just lowered its shoulder some more, as if realizing how small Tim was. He realized Riina hadn't stayed behind him.

"Give me a boost," she said.

He sighed, and cupped his hands, lowering them so she could put her foot in. He used his cybernetic boost to propel her up on the back of the avian, then crouched and jumped, using the same boost.

He landed neatly behind the avian's head. It was unsettling, to say the least. He could feel the ripple of muscles under the feathers, his sensors registered its living warmth. This close, it disturbed him to see the dirty grayness of its feathers. This was no place for any living creature, let alone this large bird.

"Hold on," he warned, as he felt the muscles bunching beneath him. Riina's arms went around his waist, and he realized there was an upside to their current situation. He had a feeling it wouldn't be wise to share this, however.

The bird lifted off, the span of its wings putting a massive shadow on the ground beneath them as they glided forward. Tim realized there was another benefit to this. He could see further and better even than when he'd been in the flyer.

As if the bird knew it, it circled the whole of the yard, its shadow finding and leaving pile after pile of broken ships and other debris that Tim couldn't identify. It seemed odd to him that anyone had taken the time to transport all this here—wherever here was—but humans did odd things for reasons he wasn't sure he'd ever understand.

His cybernetics found and mapped the shuttle's flight, while sending data of their progress back to it. It could only benefit the shuttle to have this information and would hopefully shorten the time it needed to be airborne and exposed while it searched for some kind of central control.

At first, it looked like a sea of messed up and damaged stuff, but finally, he thought he saw something that might have been a building. When the bird angled direction toward the area, and so did the shuttle, he wondered if their destinations were the same? But then T'Korrin peeled off and landed on the building and they went on.

Great. Their one source of communications had left them.

As the bird began to glide lower, he realized there was another area that could be buildings. In any other situation, he might have found it amusing that it was so hard to tell habitations from junk, but he was flying on the back of a large bird. It robbed him of the ability to be amused.

The bird landed on the top of the building and gave a loud cawing sound. Tim checked his tracking. The shuttle was at the other location. The possibly enemy craft was hovering closer, while still keeping its distance.

"I am attempting to jack into their systems," Trac said.

Tim winced. "Be…"

"Careful. I know. Veirn is assisting."

Now their ride lowered its shoulder again. Tim took this as an invitation to dismount. He clasped Riina's arm and swung her down to the ground, then jumped down, landing lightly beside her.

It wasn't ideal being on the roof. It was flat with several vents poking up from the surface. As far as he could tell, there was no egress point up here. But, after he'd paced the perimeter, he realized there was no other landing place for the bird.

"We need to get down," he said.

Rinna held out her hand. He didn't like lowering her somewhere he hadn't checked out. He sighed, and acquiesced to her silent request. Riina could take care of herself. For the most part. He jumped down beside her. It was a jolt, but within his ability to cushion the landing. He was glad it wasn't any higher, however.

This side of the building was a blank slate, so he led the way around, finding another blank side—not even windows broke the surface—but on the third side they found an entrance.

The rusted hatch wasn't impressive. What was in there that the avian wanted them to rescue?

He tried the handle. It wasn't a surprise to find it secured. He studied the lock and then tried a power surge. If it didn't work—

It did. It still took extra boost to slide it back. Inside lights came on automatically revealing a dismal scene that matched the exterior. Rusted metal cages lined the walls on three sides. all were empty, which was a puzzle. There was a console, perhaps a security station?

Riina went to this and studied the controls.

"I think there is more underground," she said.

He joined her. He'd seen controls like these before. After a brief hesitation—his mind on that *Q'uy* ship—he punched in using his cybernetics. The connection was slower than he was used to. This was an old system, old even by his standards.

It was also in an unfamiliar language. He tried triggering controls and after a couple of attempts, a hatch slid open just behind the control station.

"You should wait here," he told Riina. When she started to object, he added, "Someone could come behind us and lock us in."

She didn't look happy, but she nodded. And she pulled her weapon, moving around the station so that the door was in clear sight.

Inside the hatch, he found lift controls. Again, not in any

language he could understand. So, he pushed something. The hatch closed between he and Riina and the lift began to lower. When it stopped and the door opened again, lights came on revealing a large cavern. It had to reach up almost to the surface, he decided.

There were more of the cages lining the walls and another control station. But these cages, he realized, weren't empty. He jacked into the control station again, and somehow managed to turn on the lights inside the cages.

Humans, animals, and one very large avian blinked at him.

He had a feeling that the avian was the Timmy in the well.

22

Riina shifted uneasily, checking the time once again. Tim had only been gone a couple of minutes. It felt like an hour. She tried comms.

"Tim?"

"Yes?"

The relief almost buckled her knees.

"Are you all right?" she asked.

"I'm not sure how to answer that question," Tim said. "I have found a prisoner cell block. I am unsure how to proceed."

"You can't let them go?"

"I am one. They are many, including another large avian."

"Timmy," she said.

"Yes."

Tim had left the console unlocked, but the language and coding was unfamilair.

She tried comms again, this time to the shuttle.

"Veirn, if I send you a video, could you help me out with this control station?"

"I could try," Veirn's fragment said cautiously.

She turned on her video feed.

"I am receiving," the AI said. A pause. "It is similar to the systems I am currently attempting to access here at what we believe is the central command center. Please wait."

Riina heard the scramble of claws on the metal ceiling and then a shadow darkened the doorway. After a few seconds, the bird's head—or the part of it with an eye—filled the doorway.

"We're working on it," she said. She looked, without touching. There had to be some kind of larger hatch entry for them to get the avian inside. That had to mean the ceiling could be raised and the floor in the center of the room must also have some kind of opening. It was the only thing that made sense.

She studied it. Yes, she was certain it had to be a large hatch, too. If only she could find the matching control. Her comms crackled, then Veirn spoke.

"I believe I have translated the controls correctly, but the only way to know for sure…" the AI stopped.

"…is to try. Let me see them," she said. The data packet arrived, and she downloaded it to her suit's systems. Then activated it and suddenly the controls made sense.

If Veirn were correct.

Her hand hovered over the upper hatch control. Then she looked at the bird.

"I'm going to open it." She pointed up. There was a pause, then the bird's head vanished. Its shadow passed over the space outside. So, it had lifted off the roof. That was good. She pushed the control.

———

"The shuttle on the surface is in motion," Veirn told Kellen.

He didn't ask what that movement might mean. How could the AI know?

So far it didn't seem as if the blockade could see them, so their cloak was working. If his ship had been equipped with phased cloaking, he'd have tried to pass through the blockade, but his ship was not equipped with the ability to pass through solid objects.

It hadn't been offered the tech, but then he hadn't asked for it. It had seemed unnecessary and risky. He'd seen video of a ship passing through another ship and the wrongness of it had given him nightmares. Now…

"Can we slip between the ships to reach the surface?" he asked.

"They are too close together for the size of our ship," Veirn said.

His people were so close. It was frustrating to have come so far to be stopped now.

"Can we make contact with our people without our signal being detected?" It would have been nice to at least let them know help was here. And with their smaller ship, they could most likely pass between the blockade ships and get to them.

"I am uncertain," Veirn said. It did not sound happy. The AI didn't like being uncertain. "Their technology, some of their technology, is unfamiliar. I have been unable to access their systems."

It had tried to access their systems? Kellen felt discomfort at the idea. He wouldn't like anyone accessing his systems without his knowledge, but…they were far from home. They had no backup. And they had people at risk and out of reach.

"How…" Kellen wasn't sure exactly how to phrase the question.

"The crew of the *Najer* had this capability and the information came with their information upload," Veirn said. "I had not planned to use the information, but…"

And there it was again. *But.*

He needed to either stop the AI or give verbal approval.

"Very well," Kellen said. "Just…do no harm," he added. And if the AI learned they were more than hostile? If doing harm was the only way to get to their people? He wanted to push the decision off until it had to be made but—and there it was again—in the heat of the situation was not the best time to decide. At least it would give him something new to think about.

"Any ideas or suggestions on how to proceed?" Kellen couldn't believe he'd said the words. He was the ship's captain. He should know or have ideas. But it wasn't unheard of to get ideas from the crew and Veirn was all the crew he had.

"I am running scenarios," Veirn said.

Kellen might be surprised it had plural scenarios to run. He could think of only two. Try to shoot their way past them. Try to talk to them.

"I suppose we could try making contact with them," Kellen said, reluctantly, presenting what felt like the lesser of two difficulties.

"I would save that as a last resort," Veirn said.

Kellen wished they had another, different last resort than trying to make contact with a large, unknown flotilla of ships.

———

The building rumbled, reminding him of the seismic activity back on Arroxan Prime. Dust filtered down from the high domed ceiling.

"Riina?" He asked.

"I have opened an outside hatch," she said. "Are you all right?"

"Yes." But the structure around him still seemed to shudder with movement. It suddenly felt urgent to make a decision about the prisoners. He still didn't like his odds. But then, they hadn't been that good since they'd been sucked into that unknown ship and then dumped here.

"Is there a secondary hatch in the floor?"

"Yes," she said. "I was going to wait…"

"Open it," he said.

He began to work the controls as he felt and saw the upper roof of the chamber begin to slide back. Its resistance told him that it hadn't been activated in a long time.

And now, at his level, doors began to release on the various cells. The humans inside looked surprised and wary. Through the opening from above, T'Korrin flew down and began to circle the chamber, calling out what sounded very much like a warning.

The last cell door—the one that caged the large avian—shuddered open. The humans who had begun peering out of their cells flinched back.

Red lights began to strobe, mixing with the pale yellow lighting.

The huge bird stepped out, lifting and flexing its wings as if it had forgotten how to use them. Perhaps it had. Its gold and red gaze swept the chamber, stopping at the sight of Tim.

His throat went dry.

Then, far above, he heard the cry of the other avian. This one lifted its head, returning the cry. Its wings began to beat the air, stirring up old dust into mini vortexes. Its massive legs bunched, and then it surged up, the wings frantically beating in its drive to rise. At the opening, it was forced to contract those wings, but it seemed as if it had enough glide force to pass through and out of sight.

Pale light now filtered down through the dust and strobing lights as the avian flew out of sight.

T'Korrin remained, reemerging to begin its frantic calling and flying around and around.

"I know," Tim said. "We need to go.

The structure began to shudder harder now, which just

seemed petty to Tim. He'd just unloaded what had to be a lot of weight.

He waved at the humans, hoping it was the right thing to do, and opened the lift hatch door.

"We have to go!" he called out, aware they probably couldn't understand him.

Now he could see stairs at each level of the prison. The humans, after some shuffling, began hurrying toward the stairs. The shaking of the various levels was probably helping to motivate them.

They scrambled down the stairs, their progress mostly orderly. This gave him hope. If anyone pushed or shoved, he'd make sure they weren't on the lift with him.

As they reached the ground floor, he directed them into the lift. They didn't look happy about it. He didn't blame them. It looked like yet another trap. But it was the only way out for those without wings.

He did a head count and some calculations. They might all make it inside. Though there were many cells, they weren't all inhabited.

There was a human woman clinging to the shaking railing as she descended the last set of stairs. A gap was growing between her and the rest of the humans. Tim left his post and ran to her, lifting her onto his back in a smooth movement that had to be a leftover memory from his time as a robot.

He felt and heard her gasp, but after a moment, her arms slid around his neck. He ran back toward the lift. They were the last ones, and the doors were starting to grind closed. He put on a burst of speed and managed to get them inside.

It didn't feel like a win when the lift began to rise in slow, jerking movements. The humans made small, distressed sounds, but no one panicked that Tim could tell.

"We're coming up," he told Riina, not sure she could hear him over the groaning protests of the failing structure.

The shaking and shuddering increased. His systems had recorded how long it took him to descend. They were close, but were they close enough?

He lowered the woman, indicating to a male human to support her, then moved to the center of the lift and looked up. There was an access hatch. He crouched and jumped, punching through the hatch, before dropping down again.

He crouched, jumped again and this time was able to catch hold of the edge and pull himself up on top of the lift. It only took a moment for him to realize that the cable was taking too much strain for its age and condition.

He grabbed it, reducing the strain, shifting that strain to his shoulders and arms and legs. Did he have enough left of the robot to do this? He wasn't sure.

He looked up, saw the hatch just above them.

"Can you open the hatch to the lift, Riina?" She hadn't answered him before. He wasn't sure why.

The lift strained upwards toward the dark rectangle.

He wasn't sure how long he could do this.

Then the hatch slid open and Riina leaned out.

The relief might have given him the needed push for the last bit.

Of course, the lift stopped just shy of the hatch. It was yet one more part of this never-ending day.

He eased his grip on the cable. It held. Just.

He leaned down, reaching his hand. At first the humans stared at him. Then one man reached up and took his hand. Tim lifted him up and out, gesturing toward the open hatch. It was a scramble for him, but doable.

After that, getting the humans to take his help got easier. One of the males, Tim noted his face for future reference, helped the injured woman up before taking Tim's help. They both boosted her up and out of the lift shaft.

The humans, Tim was glad to see, had already evacuated the

building. He could see some of them still making their way around the huge gap in the floor where the hatch had been.

"Run. Get out of here," he told Riina, urging her ahead of him as he once more put the injured female on his back. He couldn't hit his top speed because of Riina and the humans ahead of him.

The shuddering and groaning increased. He guessed the structure was about to collapse in on itself. How far would the impact reach outside? Had the humans evacuated far enough?

Outside he found the avians and the canines herding the humans away from the site.

Tim didn't have time to blink at the sight. He'd have to blink later. Now that they were outside, he could hook an arm around Riina's waist and pick up the pace, his cybernetics boosting arms and legs.

It felt as if the ground were crumbling behind them. He didn't dare to even look back, and it wasn't until he was well clear that he remembered that his cybernetics could have, possibly had, recorded the event.

His single focus shocked him. But he didn't have time to worry about that either.

If his head count was correct, they'd acquired at least another ten humans.

The woman struggled against him, and he stopped and lowered her to the ground. They were clear of the collapse, but only just. But now one of the large avians dropped lightly down in front of them, as if it knew not to slam into the ground.

The female limped slowly toward it, and it lowered its head and gently pressed it against her.

"I think," Riina said, "they know each other."

Now he noticed what he hadn't noticed before about her. She was haggard and thin, dirty hair hanging around pale, purple skin. He wasn't sure why that surprised him. He'd seen many strange things in his travels, but he couldn't recall a purple alien.

His radio crackled once, then again. He heard Lt. Dish's voice.

"How is Timmy?"

For a moment, Tim couldn't think what she was talking about. And then, impossibly, he chuckled.

"Timmy is no longer in the well."

23

Riina still found her mind struggling with the idea of the birds and the canines going from adversaries to protectors, but that is what her eyes told her had happened.

The canines had formed a protective barrier around the freed prisoners.

It was completely awkward and frustrating that they couldn't communicate with each other. The rescued prisoners stared at them. Some even spoke. She shrugged helplessly and told them she didn't understand.

They probably didn't understand that. It made her realize how much she'd relied on their tech to do things. The skills that real first contact required had been lost or left behind a long time ago.

Without the shuttle, without their ship, they were left with hand signals.

At least they had to know they'd rescued them. That they probably weren't bad guys.

"We could probably transport the people," Rinna said, "if we had the *Quendala*. We might even could fit them in the shuttle for a short time." A short and highly uncomfortable time.

"If we knew where we were going," Tim pointed out.

It was a big if, no question. She could only hope that Trac and Veirn's fragment were finding that out.

"But the avians and the canines? I feel fairly certain that they are prisoners here, too. How do we save them?"

That earned a look from Tim that she generously called surprised and not incredulous.

Yes, she knew that none of the larger non-humans could fit on the *Quendala*. That didn't relieve them of their responsibility to help them. She didn't say this. Tim could rightly point out that right now they couldn't even save themselves.

Their contact with the shuttle at the moment was limited. They'd had contact long enough to be told that they were working on accessing the systems of the facility without getting Trac's brain taken over. At least, that is how Lt. Dish had explained it.

A large canine, the leader of the pack, Riina decided, as she studied it, approached them. Its head was lowered enough to signal—she hoped—non-aggression. It stopped some feet away and extended a paw. It had the same kind of electronic device as the avian had worn.

"You know that thing is probably controlling it," Tim muttered. He sighed and then went up to it, kneeling to examine it.

Riina saw a flash, like the one that had freed the avian, and the device dropped to the ground.

In short order, the whole pack came over to be freed and finally the other large avian.

What Riina noticed, or thought she noticed, was that they had humans, birds, and wolves who were all hungry and thirsty and in need of medical care. Even the animals had wounds.

And then, because things weren't strange enough, a flyer came into view, its movements as jerky and uncoordinated as the first flyer that had brought the doughy alien to meet them.

"Oh, that can't be…" she began.

But it was. Only this flyer was armed.

———

"Something is happening with the blockade," Veirn said, breaking a long period of silence.

Kellen had used the time to—reluctantly—consume some real food. He'd felt emptiness gnawing at his ability to focus and had addressed the issue, even though each bite had been like eating dust.

This had necessitated leaving the bridge. Now he headed back at a run. He could almost hear his past captains admonishing him that captains didn't run.

This one ran.

He skidded onto the bridge and grasped the back of his seat, trying to catch his breath and see what had changed. He hadn't, he realized, asked if the change was for the better. Looking at the screens, he'd have been hard-pressed to choose between better or worse.

"They are moving," he muttered. He came around and dropped into his chair, changing the settings on one screen to get a different view. "Their formation appears to be contracting."

"The formation is descending into atmosphere."

Kellen examined this information from as many sides as his tired brain could come up with. And ended up back at better or worse. Which was it?

"If they start attacking the surface…" he began.

"I will initiate contact with the shuttle," Veirn said.

"We should close the distance," Kellen said. "If the shuttle can evacuate…" Kellen knew he didn't have to explain to the AI why closer was better.

"Yes, Captain," Veirn said.

Kellen blinked. The AI hadn't exactly been following protocol for some time now. He wondered what the change meant.

"Is it possible that the shuttle is damaged?" Kellen felt his insides tighten at this thought. They'd seen signs of it transiting from one location to another, but that didn't mean it hadn't taken damage. "We have another shuttle. I could…"

"It would be unwise for you to leave the ship, Captain," Veirn said.

It hadn't reminded him of regulations—though as one of his human friends had said once, when this far from normal, regulations were really just guidelines.

"I can deploy the shuttle to the surface."

Veirn could also pilot this ship without its captain, Kellen wanted to point out. But there was something to be said for keeping the human factor in play when facing so much that was unknown. Of course, sending the shuttle away left them with only escape pods if something went very wrong. He suppressed a shudder at the thought. They were too close in size to the sleep pod he'd gone into so long ago.

"Do it," Kellen said.

"Yes, Captain."

———

"We have incoming," Trac said over comms.

Tim stiffened, his gaze going upwards. At first, even his cybernetics couldn't see anything but the murk that seemed to be a feature of this dismal place. He just had time to wonder if the flyer had registered the incoming, when a line of bright line stabbed down and took out the flyer, leaving only bits of falling debris where it had been.

"That was handy," Riina said.

"I hope so," Tim said. The enemy of one's enemy wasn't necessarily one's friend. At least in his experience.

If the non-humans and humans had been concerned by the flyer, they hadn't had time to show it. Now they looked up, the expressions in their haggard faces turning eager.

Tim glanced around, looking for a place for them to retreat to, but they had the crater at their back and the rescued prisoners between them and any good cover.

Now he could see the flare of ships entering the atmosphere. It didn't take long. Whatever this place was, it wasn't a planet, he didn't think. A sort of way station? It was possible.

The rounded bottoms of multiple discs emerged from the flares. They varied in size, but not in shape. The larger of them moved toward their location and then slowly settled above them.

No, mostly above the others. All of them looked up now, waving as well as they could in their weakened conditions. Some of them hugged.

"I guess they know who it is," Riina said. She glanced back, but must have realized, as he had, that they had no where to go.

The large avian and the female human began to speak to the others. They shuffled toward her and some of them helped to boost her up onto the avian's back. Then half of them scrambled up there, too. The avian lifted off and the other one landed, so that the rest of the humans could climb on.

"What about the canines?" Riina wondered.

They watched as the two avians flew up to the belly of the ship, saw it open to receive them.

"Well, that solves part of the transportation problem," Riina muttered.

Tim wanted to step closer to, slide his arm around her waist, but he needed to keep his hands free, just in case.

"Why don't you stand behind me?" he murmured.

"I don't think either of us should move," Riina murmured back.

He couldn't argue with that, though he would have liked to.

The bottom of the large disc closed, and it lifted away to be replaced by a much smaller disc. This one pressed in closer. The side opened and a ramp slid down. The canines all trotted up this ramp. When Tim and Riina were alone, the ramp pulled in, and the hatch closed once more.

"Now what?" Tim muttered, as this ship lifted away from them.

"They could have said hello," Riina said. "Or thank you."

Tim thought about the haggard, purple female. She will tell them, he thought. But yes, it would have been nice if they could have gotten star charts from them. But that would have told these unknown aliens how vulnerable they were. It was clear that the aliens in the ships had trust issues. Well, so did they.

The ships were rising, interacting with the thin atmosphere again. So many flares. So many ships. Would they ever know the story of this place?

"They are leaving," Trac said, unnecessarily over the comms.

"They are jumping away," came Kellen's voice, his relieved voice, over their comms.

"Captain?" Tim was surprised he could get the word out. His was the last voice he'd expected to hear over the comms.

"How did you find us?" Riina said.

"It is a long story. Let's get you all back on board and then we can talk."

"Do you know the way home?" Tim had to ask it.

"Yes, well, Veirn knows the way home."

And now Tim did turn to hug Riina. If they'd dared to lift their faceplates, he'd have kissed her.

24

The shuttle materialized in front of them, not quite resting on the unstable ground. She and Tim had needed to move further away from the crater they'd helped create, as the ground kept shifting and shuddering.

"It was," Tim said, "like being back on Arroxan Prime."

They'd shared a grin, but more than the grin was the look of promise in his eyes. His gaze was like the one in her dreams. Intent, focused, filled with love.

When they went up the ramp, she was surprised to find the rear bay empty.

"This is the other shuttle," Tim said, glancing around. He grinned again. "We're alone."

Riina grinned back and then had to bite back a yawn. "Sorry."

He looped an arm around her waist. "You need food and rest in that order."

Tim waited until Riina was settled into the fold down bunk, taking just a moment to look at her lying there with her lashes making half-moons on her pale cheeks. This had been a rough one and it wasn't over yet.

Arroxan Prime was still out there and their first contact mission. But for now, they were headed back to the *Quendala*.

He headed for the cockpit and settled into the pilot's seat. Yet another fragment of Veirn was piloting the shuttle, but he felt the need to monitor their progress—and that of the other shuttle.

As the strange junkyard began to fall way behind them, he could see it better now.

It was what he'd loosely call a space station, though it was more platform than anything. Wide and flat and messed up in every way he could think of.

There'd been no other life signs. So, the pilot who had tried to help him was dead, too, or had been lifted away by the aliens? That was possible.

The large alien and his side kick were definitely dead. And the myriad of smaller aliens that had attacked him?

No sign of any of them.

He wondered if anyone would come after them, perhaps to leave a derelict ship, and find a ghost station, or if some other nasty human would move in and take it over.

He wasn't sorry he might not never know. He'd be happy to never come here again.

25

With an echo of the sense of 'been here, done this,' Kellen stood in his bay as first one, then another shuttle landed. The people that began to straggle out appeared shell-shocked, relieved, worried, afraid, and possibly just a little excited.

"It's my first spaceship," one woman muttered, looking around with awe.

But they were all also exhausted and though they hadn't starved yet—the supplies on the shuttle had been enough to keep them going but they'd been rationed and running out—they were hungry for real food.

His people looked as strained as they each were capable of. Trac, of course, didn't look like anything but himself.

But there were his people—crew and rescued—and it appeared they picked up a bird along the way. The strain of the last week showed clearly on their faces. Even Lt. Dish was missing all of her perkiness. She dragged down the ramp and gave him a wan smile that he suspected even a bowl of popcorn couldn't help.

"What do you want more?" He asked. "Food or sleep?"

She paused, and it appeared to take almost more effort than she had energy for, to try to decide.

"Go get some rest," he said.

She nodded. Kellen looked at Trac, nodding toward her and the cyborg went to her, picked her up and strode out. The lieutenant didn't even squeak a protest. It was possible she was already asleep.

Riina also looked hammered, but oddly content. Kellen glanced at Tim and thought he detected the same subtle contentment in his eyes. Had they finally both realized their feelings for each other? While he didn't want to be captain of a love ship, it was nice to see that they'd finally found each other.

Still, both of them also showed signs of strain and exhaustion. But he needed their help to deal with the Arroxan Prime people who had somehow ended up with them. He couldn't wait to hear that story.

———

It felt like it took forever to feed and settle their Arroxan Prime guests. Now that they knew they were safe — Riina didn't point out that safety was relative when you were hurtling through space using a star drive — they'd become almost cheerful. And extremely curious.

They also found, according to Lt. Dish, their whine-one-one buttons.

But they'd been tucked in at last, and Riina had been able to both eat and get some rest. She woke when she felt them drop out of star drive and made her way to the bridge as quickly as she could get ready.

Tim was already there. Had he rested at all, she wondered? There were tired lines around his eyes and mouth, but he smiled when he saw her come in.

"We've just arrived in the Arroxan Prime system," Tim told her. "We'll reach the planet in six ship's hours."

"We were able to transit back quickly because we knew the route," Veirn explained.

"We collected a lot of new data while looking for you," Captain Kellen said.

He looked tired, too. She almost said something but stopped herself. He was the captain. He'd get rested when he felt like it was the right time.

"We had something interesting happen," Kellen added. He leaned forward and manipulated some controls. An image popped up on the forward screen.

"Is that…" Riina began as she stared at a much healthier looking purple alien female.

"We believe so," Tim said.

"It is a message of thanks," Veirn said.

"How do we know?" Riina listened, but all she could hear was the same alien sounds they heard at the junk yard.

"It arrived with both prime numbers and music as part of its coding," Veirn explained. "I could, of course, have translated it incorrectly if their prime numbers were different than ours, but since you saved her life, we can reasonably assume certain things about the message. And she is smiling."

Riina grinned at Tim. "I think it is reasonable to assume it isn't a death threat."

"That," Tim said, grinning back, "is new in my experience."

Riina felt a stab of pleasure that he could joke about his dark past.

"There is more," Tim said.

"More?" Was this the bad news of the good news, bad news scenario?

"I have been able to pick up the news telecasts from Arroxan Prime," Veirn said.

That seemed like good news? She hoped. There were people alive to make those broadcasts.

"The damage to the planet is much less severe than we expected, based on our readings and observations at the time," Veirn said.

"In fact," Kellen said, "their seismic disruptions have been reduced to levels more typical of similar planets in our systems. It is possible that the sensors were originally installed because the seismic activity as so a-typical."

"It did seem," Tim observed, "that the entity was targeting high seismic regions."

"And from what Dr. Walker reported, their people didn't settle in those areas," Riina said.

"In addition," Veirn said, "they built resilient structures, so the damage from the extractions was manageable."

"Extraction?" Riina's voice might have squeaked some at this characterization.

"It is now clear that the entity extracted the Vorthari," Veirn said.

"But how…"

"They sent the Arroxan Prime government a bill," Kellen said dryly. "In their language and currency."

"A bill?" Riina's voice definitely squeaked this time. "And how are they supposed to pay it?"

"If the news sources are correct," Veirn said, "they already have taken payment. They also extracted some minerals while they were here."

"Very valuable minerals," Kellen said, "but their seismic problem is solved, so they seem to think it is worth it."

Riina blinked, as she considered this information. "So we came to help with their Vorthari problem…"

"..these aliens solved it for us," Tim confirmed.

"But," Riina frowned in puzzlement, "how did they know to come? Who hired them?"

"According to sources inside the government," Veirn said, "someone called Pollin Sollin sent them a message."

There was a short silence, then Riina said, her tone almost hushed, "Do you think he knew what he was doing?"

"I'm going to go with…" Tim said, "not a clue."

Rinna smiled at his use of the Earth term.

Another short silence ensued. Kellen cleared his throat.

"I could be wrong," Kellen said, "but I think our first contact problem is also moot. Without our intervention, they have learned they are not alone in the universe."

She exchanged a look with Tim that was decidedly rueful as she mentally checked that mission priority box off, too. It was hard not to feel like their dash to the rescue had been a little embarrassing.

The only thing left for them to do was to return their accidental guests to their planet. And find out what Dr. Walker wanted to do about his side chick.

————

Tim had a strange moment of disconnect as he took a seat in the small conference room of the *Quendala*. There was no Doc, General Halliwell, or the Maestra, of course. Instead, they had Dr. Walker, his side chick, Lira Taan, her father, Riina, and Captain Kellen.

"How are your people doing?" Kellen asked Dr. Taan.

"Truthfully?" Dr. Taan ran hands through his hair, causing some disruptions in its flatness. "They will be glad to get home. They are finding space travel…unsettling."

Veirn had arranged for them to see streams of the various news broadcasts, so they all knew their planet was safe, and in some ways better off. They'd also seen reactions to the alien extraction event—as they were calling it.

Tim suspected that they were taking it as well as they were

because there was no one to complain to about it. The aliens had come, extracted a threat they hadn't known was there, and left with their seismic problem mostly solved.

All that was left for them was acceptance.

Dr. Taan's lips twitched slightly before he added, "In other circumstances they might have had some exciting alien abduction stories to share, but it's pretty clear that no one is going to care. Everyone has an alien story now. And to tell the truth, none of them ever included a space trip to, what did you call it, a junk yard in their expectations of alien contact."

"It was more than they wanted," Lira agreed.

"So basically," Dr. Walker said, "your problems are all solved."

Except for what to do about Dr. Walker, Tim thought. But it was Riina who put it into words.

"And what about you, Dr. Walker?"

Walker and Lira exchanged glances. Then he looked at Riina.

"I'd like to stay. They have a whole bunch of new geology for me to explore and map. And…" he looked at Lira, his gaze softening. "The fact that I'm an alien, well, even Drun doesn't think it will matter. With the alien autopsy off the table…"

"Are you sure? We might not get back your way in your lifetime," Riina said. "This is—or was—a quiet corner of the universe."

"I'm cool with it," Walker said.

His hand covered Lira's that was resting on the tabletop and they exchanged a look that was weighted with much intent. Tim was rather proud of himself that he recognized it.

"You don't have any desire to travel the stars, Lira?" Tim asked. He found this all rather baffling. Even as a slave, he had liked going and doing and seeing other planets and systems. It is what had made the dark part of it bearable.

"I never did," Lira said. "It was my father who was all about the aliens. I'm an archeologist with a lot of new ground to explore, too."

Tim looked at Dr. Taan.

"But I wasn't looking *up* for aliens," Dr. Taan pointed out. "I always knew the aliens were below us. And now, at least everyone knows now that I wasn't crazy." He glanced around. "This is appealing. This ship, this type of travel. I won't lie, but my family is on Arroxan Prime, and I've already spent too much time away from them. I am content to go home."

Words, Tim realized. Somehow, through it all, they'd solved the biggest problems with words. He might be—what was that word that Colonel Carey liked to use?—gobsmacked. Was that it? It sounded like what he felt. Gobsmacked.

———

Pollin Sollin stood in the shadow of the trees watching as the rest of his people walked down the shuttle's ramp. It felt good to have Arroxan Prime land under his feet again. He was, he could admit in this brief space of quiet, struggling to process all that had happened.

He'd gone to meet aliens.

And he had. Eventually.

And then everything had gone wrong. Because of aliens, just not because of the aliens he'd hoped to meet.

Instead of a photo opportunity and possible fame, he'd been abducted. He'd been forced to eat alien emergency food so he wouldn't starve. There had been moments he'd wanted to starve.

Mostly, he sighed as he faced it, he'd been bored. They'd been shut in the back of a shuttle for—he had no idea how long. There'd been no windows to look out of, no way to mark the time. It had passed.

They'd been "rescued." From shuttle he'd gone to a space

ship. He'd had hope, but the food had still been awful. And again, no outside view.

They had been provided them with video from Arroxan Prime so they could see what had happened while they were gone. So they could see what they'd missed.

He'd flown into outer space and the only people who might have been interested in his story had been with him. They were all a non-story.

They'd all missed the main event and had a terrible view for the event they hadn't missed.

It was...ironic.

He sighed and headed toward the lights of Lira Taan's house wondering what to do now.

———

The drop-off was quiet, totally without fanfare, at the site of Lira's habitation. Riina insisted on giving Dr. Walker a beacon he could use to contact them in case of an emergency. If two sets of aliens had found them, it was possible others might as well. He thanked them, took Lira's hand, and walked into the shadows after the others.

Drun had given them stiff verbal thanks, while his gaze remained suspicious. He hadn't enjoyed the unexpected ride, and he'd had a better view than most about what they'd been up against, so Riina didn't fault him for a lack of graciousness.

Dr. Taan ran a hand down the side of the shuttle, gave a sigh, and then turned and walked after his daughter.

That left Riina and Tim alone in the quiet dark. They didn't speak as they walked up the ramp. It closed behind them, thanks to Veirn's fragment, which was still hanging around. It was not a surprise that Veirn had trust issues about Arroxan Prime.

They went to the cockpit, but Tim let Veirn pilot the ship

back to the *Quendala*. He was deeply tired in a way that he assumed was typical of being human, but also happy in a way he'd never been able to achieve as a cyborg.

He lowered his faceplate and pulled off his gloves. Riina followed suit, and they clasped hands as the shuttle lifted off the surface.

"Do we know how long it's been…" Riina began, then shook her head.

Did it matter, she seemed to indicate? He could be agree. It been long enough and that is what mattered.

———

Thank you for reading *OmnitronW!* The next book in the series will be *TalusH* coming in 2026!

I know it's hard to wait, so here's a bonus epilogue you can get for free, just by signing up for my newsletter. Just click here to get your free epilogue!

To find out about all my releases, be sure to sign up for my Newsletter and get a free eBook when you do. You can also find out more by visiting my website.

If you enjoyed this book, I hope you'll consider leaving a review. It's not just because I'm needy (even though I try not to be!). Reviews help other readers decide which books to buy. :-)

BOOKS BY PAULINE BAIRD JONES

Science Fiction Romance/Paranormal

Project Enterprise: The Cyborg Chronicles
    Cyborg's Revenge: The Cyborg Chronicles Book 1
    Cosmic Boom: The Cyborg Chronicles Book 2
    CabeX: The Cyborg Chronicles Book 3
    AzumC: The Cyborg Chronicles Book 4
    MircoP: The Cyborg Chronicles Book 5
    ScytheQ: The Cyborg Chronicles 6
    OmnitronW: The Cyborg Chronicles 7
    TalusH: The Cyborg Chronicles 8
    TrackerY: The Cyborg Chronicles 9

Project Universe Series:
    The Key (book 1)
    Girl Gone Nova (book 2)
    Tangled in Time (book 3)
    Steamrolled (book 4)
    Kicking Ashe (book 5)

The Reboot Books of Project Enterprise
Found Girl (book 6)
Lost Valyr (book 7)
Maestra Rising (book 8)
More Project Enterprise
Project Enterprise: The Short Stories
Time Trap: A Project Enterprise Series Short Story
Operation Ark: A Project Enterprise Story
General's Holiday: A Project Enterprise Story
Claws & Effect: The Otherworldly Pets of Project Enterprise

Other Romantic Science Fiction Stories
The Real Dragon
Nebula Nine (time travel adventure)
Open With Care (Christmas collection that includes, "Riding For Christmas" and "Up on the House Top"
Specters in the Storm: A paranormal/steampunk/science fiction romance novella

Out of Time Series:
Out of Time
Just in Time
Telling Time
Out of Time Series (Three Book Bundle)

An Uneasy Future
(A science fiction romance mystery series set in future New Orleans)
Core Punch (1.0)
Sucker Punch (2.0)
One Two Punch: An Uneasy Future Bundle

Romantic Suspense

The Big Uneasy Series:
  Relatively Risky (1)
  Family Treed (A Big Uneasy Short Story)
  Dead Spaces (2.0)
  Louisiana Lagniappe (3.0)
  Worry Beads (4.0)
  Fais Do Do Die (5.0)
  Beaucoup Fracas (6.0)
  Pirogue Wipe Out (7.0)
  Bourre Brouhaha (8.0)
  Soc Au' Lait Stiff (9.0)
  Gumbo Ya-Ya Exit (10.0)
  The Family Way (A Big Uneasy Short Story)
  Guess Who's Coming To Christmas: The Wedding Edition
  The Big Uneasy Bundle
  An Uneasy Collection: The Big Uneasy Books 3-5

Lonesome Lawmen Series:
  The Last Enemy
  Byte Me
  Missing You
  Lonesome Mama (Bonus short story)
  (The *Lonesome Lawmen* is also available as a digital bundle)

Do Wah Diddy Die
  The Spy Who Kissed Me
  *Perilously Fun Fiction Bundle (*includes *The Spy Who Kissed Me* and *Do Wah Diddy Die.* Bonus: *Do Wah Diddy Delete Short Story Collection)*
  Dangerous Dance
  Dangerous Duet

Short Story Collections

Project Enterprise: The Short Stories
    Do Wah Diddy Delete
    Let's Fall in Love
    The Real Dragon and other short stories

ABOUT THE AUTHOR

Award-winning author Pauline Baird Jones writes *perilously fun fiction*—from romantic suspense to space opera, time travel and more. With 40+ books, a flair for humor, and a love of adventure, she creates heroines braver than they realize and heroes brave enough to love them. If you crave thrilling plots, smart laughs, and happy endings, you're in the right place! 🚀🤍📖

To find out more about Pauline or her books:
http://paulinebjones.com

www.ingramcontent.com/pod-product-compliance
Lightning Source LLC
Chambersburg PA
CBHW070703280626

47159CB00022B/1867